Life Within Parole

VOLUME 2

ROANNA SYLVER

To everyone whose story feels stuck in its darkest hour,
hanging on tight and earning their happy ending.

Content Notes

Thought and Memory: Brief mentions of parental abuse/family dysfunction

Recognition: Kidnapping/imprisonment, allusion to torture, ableism

Words: Grief/loss, mentioned past character death

Life Returns: Non-damaging body horror/Zilch repairs

Happening Again: Kidnapping/imprisonment, torture, needles, implications of sexual assault, drugs, drugging without consent, brief loss of bodily autonomy (Hans)

Withdrawal: Drug withdrawal, hallucinations, medical peril, discussion of possible deaths

Always Be You: Mildly NSFW; non-explicit sexual arousal, discussions of orientations/boundaries

Stitches: Non-damaging body horror/more Zilch repairs

Memento Ignis: Funeral processes, burning of a shrouded body, discussion of death/SkEye's institutional horrors

You're Not Going That Way: Guns, body and psychological horror (ghosts being unsettling), PTSD/autistic near-meltdown. Major character death.

ONE WEEK BEFORE CHAMELEON MOON

Liam loved the smell of books. There was something about the distinctive aroma of printer's ink on aged paper he found instantly calming, in a way little else could match. Liam wasn't often calm, or happy, but these days, he was starting to come close.

The library was a hotspot for Parole activity, and while most of its patrons had the sense to keep some semblance of quiet in the ever-chaotic city, he still did everything he could to avoid them. Liam had no patience for noisy, unhygienic crowds tramping up and down the shelves, smearing sooty fingerprints on clean pages, and putting books

But he did have one precious oasis. A reading room in the back, small compared to the library's open main floor. The older, more fragile—or potentially valuable—items were stored here, safe from further smoke damage, or wayward, dog-earing fingers.

The collection was modest but beautiful, even he had to admit. Whoever had saved these mostly hardcover editions from the fires of Parole had done a good job of preserving and keeping them safe where, by all rights, they should have been the first thing to go up in smoke.

Liam could easily spend hours in here, carefully leafing through volumes on small-plant botany, naval history and strategy, and a plethora of other subjects that would have absolutely no use in Parole. He had a special, irony-tinged appreciation for some of the more dystopian titles. Orwell, Bradbury, and Huxley's famed (and ignored) literary warnings had clearly seen a great deal of page-turns, most recently his.

But if he wanted socio-political commentary, all he had to do was look out a window or take a breath. Parole was a living, smoke-breathing example of times that past modern-day seers had warned against. But even if all their bodies were inexorably imprisoned, Liam still had somewhere to turn for an escape of the mind.

There was poetry even in Parole. His eyes traveled over lines of words that, like the people here, had survived the one-city apocalypse. His mouth moved soundlessly, feeling out consonants, alliteration, rhythm. He was so absorbed he didn't hear the door open. He probably wouldn't have heard an explosion outside. But he did hear a familiar voice.

"Hey there, Wednesday! How you doing?"

"Full of woe," Liam said, but smiled. He didn't need to look up to know Ash had a smile on his face, one it had taken him a while to earn the privilege of seeing.

"Huh?" By the time Liam actually looked up, a look of confusion had replaced Ash's smile. It reminded him of an otherwise-clever dog stymied by some human-made device, and he suppressed a chuckle. It wouldn't fit with the rest of him.

"The old rhyme, Wednesday's child is full of woe?" He raised his eyebrows, and Ash shook his head.

"Uh, I was thinking of another Wednesday," Ash said, a slightly embarrassed look coming over his face. It was even better than his confusion. Strangely, he snapped twice with both hands, then looked even more sheepish when Liam mirrored his earlier perplexed expression. "She wears a lot of black too. Uh, hey, that's a good one!"

Ash pointed at the book in Liam's hands, clearly wanting to change the subject.

"You've read it?"

If it were anyone else, Liam might have been embarrassed by today's reading material: 19th-century poetry, but nothing Liam had ever heard of, works or writers. The cover read *The Cage Of My Heart Lies In Ruin*, above a stylized illustration of a birdcage, door open, with a heart inside. Beneath the cage, a pair of ravens flew free, leaving black feathers in their wake.

"I live here," Ash said with a laugh, holding up his arms to indicate the shelves, the walls that made up the library's bones. "Don't look so surprised."

"It's just that I wouldn't have thought it was your taste," Liam said carefully. It wasn't that he was looking to offend his—was friend the right word? Even in a world of books, Liam had a hard time picking one word to describe Ash and himself. But he also couldn't see Ash, with his easy social graces, many friends, and muscular frame sitting around here with his nose in any book, much less one containing admittedly flowery poetry.

"Eh, I think there's a lot of good you can get out of stuff that isn't a hundred percent your usual type." Ash shrugged, a fluid and relaxed movement Liam, with his ramrod-straight spine and shoulders, would never be able to duplicate. "And a lot of those poems are about—well, the name's a good example. The cage in ruins, but it's not a bad thing, because it lets the birds escape. I think it's like, sometimes something has to break before you can be free and make your own life."

"That's exactly how I interpreted it," Liam said, and now a faint smile crept onto his face. Smiling without intending to was always surprising, and he never did it anywhere but here. But then he hesitated, and his smile flickered and died. "Ah, may I borrow it?"

"It's a library," Ash said, blinking at him in apparent surprise.

"Well, yes," Liam acknowledged, but still didn't feel completely at ease. "I just didn't want to... presume."

"This place is here for everyone." The warmth in Ash's voice would have been clear even without looking at his face, but Liam did anyway.

"That means you too."

"I... thank you. It's just that no one's ever..." He cleared his throat. "Thank you. For this, and for letting me spend time here."

"Nobody's *letting* you do anything," Ash said, a little more firmly. "We're not going to keep somebody out who needs a safe place—hell, anyone who just wants to read. I'd say that's you more than most people."

"It is." Liam smiled, running his hands over the book's cover, spine, page edges. "I wish I could read every word ever written. I wish I could somehow—I don't know, instantly absorb the knowledge into my brain, and then keep doing that for every new book that comes. You probably think that sounds foolish."

Ash shook his head as Liam shot him a concerned glance. "Nah, not at all. I mean, I've never just devoured books like—like some people," he said, and his brief falter was not lost on Liam. "And sure, I like to kick ass and drive fast. But you gotta appreciate stuff that stays even after everything else is gone. I mean, look at Parole. Tomorrow we could all fall into that gaping fiery crater, but if someone writes about us, tells our story, then the world will know we were here, yeah?"

"That's right," Liam said softly. A shiver swept down his spine, but instead of feeling chilled, he felt warm in a way that had nothing to do with the inferno below them. "That's exactly right. Someone has to tell the truth. Someone has to keep memories alive."

Ash gave him a smile, but it was different from his usual crooked, confident grin. Smaller, slower. He almost seemed tentative, as Liam so often was when they spoke. It was strange to see on Ash' face, when Liam couldn't imagine him being hesitant or afraid of anything. But then, he hadn't figured Ash would appreciate the written word either, the stability and connection words brought, beacons of refuge amongst life's most turbulent seas.

"Hey," Ash said after a moment, and his voice was different as well, quieter than Liam generally heard it, gentler. "Just thought of another nickname for you. Raven."

"Nevermore," Liam said with a slight note of self-aware sarcasm. He held up the poetry book with its twin ravens, heart, and cage. "Or do you mean today's literature?"

"Neither," Ash said. "Random trivia time—we got the word 'Wednesday' from 'Odin's Day.' In all the stories, Odin hangs out with a couple of ravens."

"How did you know that?" Liam had to ask, genuinely impressed.

Instead of answering, Ash held up his hands again and looked up toward the ceiling. *Library*. Of course.

"Huginn and Muninn. Thought and Memory," Liam said quietly. "I... thank you. I've had quite enough of the latter. And sometimes the former is hard to accept."

"Yeah. Pegged you for that the second you walked in here," Ash said, voice still low, as if expecting some irritated librarian to shush them. "Knowing stuff no one should know, hard past, living through stuff no one should have to—even in the Turret house. Hell, maybe especially there. Don't have to be book-smart to see you didn't actually come here looking for Parole's secret rebel headquarters. You just wanted some peace and quiet."

"I did, yes." It came out almost in a whisper. "And I found it. Thanks to you."

"And if I'm right, you..." Ash gave a soft laugh, and Liam's heart ached at the warm, fond sound, at knowing it was just for him. "You will never, *ever* admit this out loud, so I'll do it for you—you wanted friends. And I hope you know, you've got at least one of those now, too."

Liam didn't know what to say. For once in his life, words failed.

So he kissed Ash before he could change his mind.

Ash was warm, all of him, always. Even in a perpetually-burning city, he seemed to give off his own aura, the kind of magnetic warmth you could feel across the room. The kind that left Liam feeling light and alive even with fires below, and turrets above. The kind that let him sleep at night. Just being near him was enough. Knowing he existed was enough. Actually kissing him, soaking in that warmth, maybe even giving him some in return...

Liam's heart beat like the wings of a bird, released to a free and open sky after a lifetime caged.

He was so lost, it took him a second to realize Ash wasn't kissing back. He wasn't pulling away, or shoving Liam away, but he wasn't kissing him back either, or embracing him, or doing anything Liam had hardly dared dream of or think possible until this moment. Apparently it wasn't possible, even now.

"I shouldn't have done that," he said quickly, stepping back in a near-panic, feeling his face flush a brilliant red. "I'm sorry. Please forgive—no, please *forget* this. I don't know what I was thinking, of course you don't—"

"No, it's not that," Ash said just as fast, and his cheeks were tinged pink as well. He looked more flustered than Liam had ever seen him, and the unprecedented, terrifying uncertainty in Ash's eyes made his stomach lurch. "You didn't do anything wrong, please don't think—I just don't want to take advantage."

"That's ridiculous," Liam protested, desperation making his words sharp. "Of course you're not."

"Yeah, but I totally could!" Ash sounded like he wanted to laugh, cry, or both. "It'd be easy. Way too easy! Listen, Wedn—Liam, we haven't known each other that long, and I don't know what exactly you've been through, but we get people who've been through Hell every day here, and I recognize enough signs to know it wasn't good! At the very least, your father..."

"The Major has no power here," Liam said when Ash trailed off, surprised at the chill in his own voice. "He has nothing to do with this place, or you—or me, not anymore."

"You're just... you're in a bad place." Ash looked like he wanted to put his hands on Liam's shoulders, but thought better of it. "And it would be easy to make that worse. A lot worse. Especially since, like I said, we haven't known each other that long, and I'm pretty sure you're falling fast and hard enough for it to hurt. And doing that, hurting you— that's the opposite of what I'm here for."

"You won't." Liam said firmly, taking one brave, maybe foolish step closer. If Ash wouldn't make the next move, fine. Liam may be mortified at being so forward after he just came to his senses, but fine. He'd tell the truth, like these words were the last story that mattered in their lives. "The only time I feel safe is when I'm here. And the only time I feel remotely... *happy*, is when *you're* here. The only time I'm *not* full of woe is when I'm here—with you. You make painful thoughts easy, and you make bad memories lose their grip."

"Liam..." It wasn't an objection or even a hesitation, not really. He knew the look in Ash's eyes, the tentative spark, the fragile hope. He didn't need a mirror to know his own eyes held the same.

"You set those ravens free." Liam reached out, and his shaking, seeking hands found both of Ash's. Big, warm, callused, nine-fingered, perfect. "I want this."

This time, Ash kissed him. When he did, Liam felt his heart break free of cages and ruins, and spread its wings.

Recognition

A VALENTINE'S DAY SPECIAL

Danae had wobbling knees, steps unsteady from one last growth spurt, and teeth that weren't used to being free of braces when the men in white put her in a room and shut the door.

The silence was pervasive. It seeped through her skin like cold water.

She'd learned the truth, and rejected the materials that made her heart sing, made her feel like her veins held light instead of blood. It wasn't worth the slaughter. Her joy would not be paid for in death.

She didn't even rage against the silence the way she had before, the

people her gifts had been used to silence.

It felt like being underwater, sinking deeper every minute. There were others here—not in her cell, never in the same room as her—but she could hear other voices, ones that sounded young, like hers. Boys maybe. She couldn't bring herself to talk to them, or even understand their words. Maybe they were talking to her, maybe not. She was lost too far below.

Until one day—or maybe night, it was so hard to tell without windows—something broke the surface. A voice, speaking directly to her, clear and nearby and without question, like a hand reaching down from an alien world of light and air.

"Hello? Is there someone else in here?"

Her answer was the first word she'd spoken in weeks. "Yeah."

They talked about all kinds of things. Favorite colors and food and family and who they'd been before they'd been locked up here, before their bodies and brains began to change too fast to track, too overwhelming to resist. About the strange place in which they found themselves now, how changed their lives were as well as their selves. About the others here—she'd been right, there were others in cells like hers. Hans, Gabriel. Too far away to speak to from here, but at least they were real, at least other people still existed outside her cage.

But the only name Danae cared about was the one belonging to the only other person her world now held. Rose, she said, laughing when she introduced herself.

"You'll get it when you see me," she said when Danae asked to be let in on the joke.

Danae didn't laugh when she was finally able to put a face to the name, one precious day when they were allowed to be in the same room for a meal.

There was a window on the opposite wall. The sunlight it let in was pale and smoky, but it lit up the flowers around the girl's face like an angel's halo.

Danae's mouth hung open, and again, she had no words.

Rose didn't laugh either. Instead, she was staring at Danae in very much the same way, like she was the miracle in the silence, and everything that had come before was noise.

When they both found their words again, they hardly stopped talking to breathe.

Rose was here for much the same reason as Danae—except she'd never even let them use her to begin with. She'd known. Been suspicious instead of naive, grown up knowing that no one who came in the name of authority promising safety and prosperity and the chance to be special was to be trusted. She didn't give them a minute of her time, or her abilities. It helped that she didn't really know how they worked herself; hardly anyone who'd taken the shot did. She might have an idea now, though. She'd had a lot of time to think.

She didn't know what had happened to her family either. Or friends. Or the whole rest of the world. (Had the barrier around Parole stayed up? Were they still cut off? Did anyone outside even know they existed? Were they really as alone out there as she and Danae were in here? Was all silence?)

The people who called themselves Radiance had given Rose her flowers, and taken everything else away.

Even her legs—no, not her original legs, she said with another of her knowing, half-laughing, half-grimacing expressions that made Danae's chest ache. Such a sweet face should never have cause to look so bitter. Her new legs, the good ones. She wasn't allowed to even take those with her, and the replacements the men-in-white gave her didn't fit right, didn't bend right, stuck and caught in the wrong places. She left them off most of the time. They were just one more thing, another reason for her to break. But she wouldn't, she said. Not ever.

Something new started to form in Danae's chest then, along with the warmth. Anger, but not for herself. And not for a faceless multitude. This suffering had a face, and she spent their entire time together trying to memorize it.

Their hands found one another after the first five minutes. They didn't let go until they had to, men in white taking them back to their individual cells, plunging them back underwater. But now Danae had a lifeline.

She called the guards that night and asked for the materials she'd rejected when she found out her crafted babies were turned into bombs. She wanted to make something, she said. She'd started to see reason. She was considering cooperating, but she was out of practice. She needed to get used to her abilities again if she was going to be any use.

The men-in-white kept a close eye on her as she worked on ankles, knees, shins and calves. She wasn't allowed to fit them to their new owner-to-be, but Danae poured all her intention of *mold, adapt, adjust, fit, cradle, comfort, embrace, empower* into the joints and small, moving parts. They would be perfect, or she'd do it again until they were.

The Radiance observers slowed her work, confiscated her project once, made her argue like a defendant in court to get them back, made her convince them she'd seen the error of her ways. Danae had always been a good liar, but never with words that stuck so painfully in her throat, promises that made her want to throw up rather than complete the sentences.

But it was worth it.

Making something good, something beautiful instead of destructive, was worth it.

Rose's smile, more radiant than any sick, banished sun, was worth it. *She* was worth it, worth everything, and always would be.

When she stole a kiss, Danae held it close to her heart, held her breath, telling the moment to last forever the way she told Rose's new legs to be perfect for her and her alone. If they were to be locked up in silence forever, she'd make this closeness last forever too. It would be her oxygen underwater; the meeting of two pieces that should never have been split, and, even here, never would be again.

Rose had just barely gotten used to her new legs, and new love, and a life that contained at least one thing that made sense when nothing else did, had just barely gotten her feet back underneath her, literally and figuratively, and had just barely begun formulating a plan—because of course she did, of course she needed one—deciding on what step to take, when, how... when all of that crumbled like dry, hollow ground.

Her cell door opened.

It wasn't Danae on the other side. It wasn't even Radiance. These men—in black, not white —wore masks, and behind one, she caught a sliver of green, scaly skin. There was a tall, shadowy figure in a hood. When she drew back in fear, it was because their arms seemed too long for the rest of them, and the voice that told her to come with them sounded more dead than alive.

But then she saw one more face she knew; one of the only other humans in this place besides Danae who hadn't been cause for alarm, for bracing herself before pain. Garrett Cole had always been kind. He'd always promised this wasn't forever, and she'd believed him the way she hadn't believed anyone else. Outside, he said, people listened when he spoke, and Rose trusted his words.

And now he told her it was time to go. When he reached out, she stepped forward toward him, and the door.

They found Gabriel next—sweet boy, he should never have been in here, it wasn't his fault, the fire that perpetually burned in him, it was the bombardment of fear and pain from other people. How much pain had Rose caused him, simply by sitting up late at night and crying? Missing her parents, her school, the birds nesting in the tree right outside her bedroom window? She had to feel it. Had to honor the pain. Danae swallowed hers, buried it. Gabriel couldn't escape the barrage.

Rose didn't know the answer—

But she knew the rush of relief when the next cell they reached was Danae's, and her hand found Rose's like it had not-nearly-enough-times before.

Like she had when she'd come here, they had to leave a life behind, and a friend with it. Sometimes she'd catch a glimpse out of the corner of her eye, a ghost boy with a sharp, crooked smile, who seemed to think every day here was a joke. Hans never let her look at him straight-on, but sometimes he'd tell her what he could see from outside. The bubble was still up, but the sky was blue beyond it. They were all trapped inside, but they were all inside together. And through it all, his smile stayed on.

Life might be just a joke, but Rose didn't feel much like laughing, she'd told him one day. Neither did he, Hans replied, but he was going to do it anyway. Somebody had to.

But Hans still wouldn't wake up, Garrett said. He'd go back for Hans, don't worry, he'll be fine. Rose nodded as he left with a bracing smile. She was so reassured, so glad they had him on their side, an adult who knew what was going on, someone they could trust. Even here, when Garret Cole spoke, people listened.

The five of them—Rose, Danae, Gabriel, the green man, and the hooded stranger—ran through smoke and searchlights; she didn't know where, but anywhere, anywhere was better than the silent room—then the ground crumbled, and swallowed Gabriel whole.

There one minute. Gone the next.

The green man was crying, the palm of one hand scorched where he'd tried to hold onto Gabriel as he fell. She still couldn't see his face, but she could see his grief in the shaking of his shoulders, the way the too-tall figure placed a too-big hand on top of his head and slowly moved it down to rest on his back.

Rose couldn't cry. You cried for things that seemed real, not nightmares. Not things that in any merciful world would reverse themselves as soon as you woke up.

Danae wasn't crying either. She was staring, but not at any of them, maybe not at anything, eyes dry, face blank. Rose was almost reminded of the day they met, when Danae had been too shocked out of her head at the sight of her to find words or blink or breathe. This was a cruel mirror, the worst distortion. This shouldn't have happened at all.

Rose would feel that pain later. Honor it. Feel horrible for being relieved, feel like a terrible, irredeemable person for being glad, unburdened, freed, that she could finally let herself cry and scream without holding back. She wouldn't worry about hurting Gabriel. There would be nothing left to hurt.

But not yet. Not now. Right now, she kept squeezing Danae's hand, the only real and solid and true thing left in the world, and kept running.

Evelyn had just gotten the hang of her new life. It was almost as changed as the rest of the world was, almost as unrecognizable—but in a much better way. In leaving one life behind, she'd found another. She'd have liked to say she didn't hesitate, but the fact was, she did; for seventeen years her life felt like nothing but one big hesitation. How did you walk away from your entire life, even if it did feel like you'd spent all of it in the space between breaths, chest aching from the exhale and not yet allowed to gasp?

Eventually she'd had enough. Liam would never forgive her for leaving (even if she'd asked him to come along, even if, for a second that would forever stretch into eternity in her memory, she saw the war being fought in his eyes, the same one she'd fought and won over her entire life, and thought he might actually say yes), but she'd never forgive herself if she stayed another second.

She met a man named Garrett Cole. When he spoke, people listened. Like they did when she sang. Like she did when he told her she'd come to the right place, that she had the makings of greatness, and even more than that, *goodness* the city so desperately needed, that she could find her place in the Emerald Bar spotlight and never be afraid again, she believed him.

There, she had everything.

She had her voice, creating her own world and all its vibrant, urgent wonders, painting herself in her own image, letting no one forget it. She could raise mountains and topple empires (and she would, just give her half a chance, just you watch; some empires *needed* toppling like she needed a cool glass of water after an extra-long set).

She had her city—and now she had the power to keep it safe, keep the thrill in her blood that told her she was on the right course, doing what she was meant to. Certainty. She'd felt it before, and never wanted to be without it again. With every hurt-in-the-making she prevented, every hurt-already-happened she helped heal, that certainty grew stronger and hardier, like a twist of green sprung up between the ash-caked sidewalk cracks.

She had her stage. It was the first place in her life that felt like home. From here, the world made sense. Even the world inside a smoking inferno-in-a-fishbowl.

Her nights were hers at last, and she'd never say she was missing anything, in no way incomplete. But you couldn't really miss something you'd never known, and once you knew, you knew.

It was hard to see much of anything in a dark house under bright lights, but she saw them. A pair of girls, their eyes shining, hands clasped as they listened, enraptured.

Evelyn sang sweeter just for them, heart telling her to listen, this was important, something truly real. The job of a performer was to find the truth in the dramatic lie, and tell it with all their heart. So she did.

When they met after the show—when she peeked out from behind the curtain to see them still in their seats in a quickly-emptying house, and thanked God she didn't have to consider strolling out to the front entrance and trying to figure out an un-creepy way of saying 'excuse me, I never do this, but when I saw you in the audience I just knew I had to talk to you, and following these instincts or impulses or whatever is the way I've built my life, trusting myself, and oh no, this really is creepy isn't it? I'm sorry, this was a mistake—'

None of that happened. Like they'd been given some signal, like they'd discussed it and planned, like a stage cue, they both looked up, and again, found her face.

Thank God again that they had the show to talk about. Evelyn had no idea what she would have said otherwise—she barely knew what she said anyway. But she'd never forget their names—Rose, Danae, of course they were. She was so strangely unsurprised. It was like hearing the lyrics to a song she knew by heart but had brain-freeze forgotten. She was able to get through that initial conversation without ruining everything. Somehow. But what she was actually feeling was much less a "hello," and more an "oh, there you are. I've been looking for you."

The next night they found one another, it felt the same. The same recognition, the same relief when they were all finally in touching distance. The feeling that they'd all been walking on uneven, brittle streets for too long, and they'd just finally stepped onto solid ground.

Evelyn felt that all-important, everlasting certainty long before they sealed the deal with two very different kisses.

One was hot and hungry, maybe a little too fast and jarring with a click of their teeth, but all the awkwardness fell away as the world spun, and her head along with it. Sometimes you just crashed into the people you were meant to be with; stranger things happened every day, and Parole was a very strange place. Once you found each other, you could take it easy—and Danae would sometimes, contrary to popular perception—but that first magnet-zap connection would never be anything but magic.

The other one was sweet and slow, both of them sighing and leaning into each other as the tension seeped out of their shoulders. It felt like slipping into a hot bath, like coming home after the day from Hell and finally closing the door and soaking in the quiet and knowing it was you, just you, except Rose was here, finally, and Evelyn never wanted her to not be here ever again.

Their lives would never be the same, and it felt like they were just beginning.

🔥

Danae, Rose, and Evelyn have seen it all.

They've seen a city rise and almost fall—*almost* because they won't let it.

As the years have gone by—fragile, frantic, blissful, never boring, always precious—they've lost friends and found them, and made new ones. Literally made one of their own, an incredible little person formed from their joined bodies and souls and shared hearts. Jack is growing and learning so fast it's dizzying. He's never seen the sky, but he sees so much more than they can even guess at sometimes. They wonder what he'll know tomorrow. They try to see the world through this sweet child's eyes, let it be new, and fresh as the bright blue sky they can barely remember.

Their lives are still not peaceful and their nights not quiet (even if two of them have left the streets behind in favor of quieter nights at home, creating, loving), but sometimes they catch glimpses of what could and will be, and look at what they already are:

Together, whole. And they smile.

Words

SIX YEARS BEFORE CHAMELEON MOON

The only thing more surprising than seeing Jay outside his usual surroundings of computers and code was almost colliding with him as he burst through a door at a flat-out run.

"Woah, hey there," Ash stammered, barely avoiding the unexpectedly high-speed crash—never the best event in a library—and falling back a few steps. "You're in a hurry. Everything okay—"

"Nothing!" Jay blurted, flushed and sweating, and cast an obviously near-panicked look at the door he'd just exited, as if expecting to be pursued by a bear, before making sure it was pulled shut behind him.

"It's nothing! Everything's fine! I don't know what you're talking about!"

With that, he blew past and tore down the hallway, scrambling around the first corner he reached, leaving Ash alone to stare after him.

There'd be no talking to Jay like this, and Ash's energy was likely to be better spent on something other than chasing down and grilling someone who clearly wanted nothing more than to hide under a rock for the rest of his natural life. There was an easier way to find out what he was dealing with, anyway. Cautiously, Ash pushed the door open and peered inside, unsure what horrible thing he expected to see, but ready for anything.

"Hi," called Regan from where he was comfortably settled in his favorite beanbag chair. He didn't seem hurt or even upset—a little stunned, if anything.

"Hi." Ash pointed one thumb over his shoulder at the door Jay had nearly ripped off the hinges. "What the hell was that? You guys' first fight?"

"No," Regan said with a slow shake of his head and bemused blink. "No, not a fight."

"So what was it?"

Regan opened his mouth, then shut it, eyes widening into an expression of dazed wonder. Then, slowly, a smile that could only be described as *dreamy* spread across his face. "It was... nice."

"Ahhh what did I do? What the hell did I do that for?" Jay was safely back in the one-room apartment he and his innermost circle called the Nerd Cave, but for once, he wasn't hard at work or play at any of the computers stacked around in varying displays of custom tinkering. He was curled in a tight, surprisingly compact ball in his swivel chair, feet on the seat and face buried in his knees. "For once couldn't I just keep my mouth shut? No, of course not, and now he's gonna hate me. Ahhh, I'm so screwed, completely fragged, that's it, man, game o—"

Knock-knock-knock.

The tapping was soft, but the already-tense Jay started anyway, half-jumping out of his skin and out of the chair, which rolled several feet back to smack into a monitor, interrupting its serene Millennium Falcon screen saver. Moving silently in his sock feet, Jay crept over to the door—the one hardly anybody ever knocked at, because if they were supposed to be here, they didn't have to knock—and stood against the wall just beside it, cursing the surveillance camera that had chosen this very morning to crap out. Like it *knew.*

"Password?" He called in a tight voice, the vocal equivalent of the cool, enigmatic pokerface he could never, ever manage in person.

"Overlord," came the muffled, slightly tentative-sounding voice from outside.

"That's last week's."

"Swordfish?"

"Week before that."

"Um... I can't rem—Jay, it's Rowan, and nobody followed me, I promise. Just open the door, please?" There was a shuffling noise outside, like hard shoe soles scraping across the floor. "I really don't like standing out here..."

"Rowan?" Jay repeated, brow furrowing in perplexed surprise, but not suspicion. He quickly undid the several locks, including a newly-installed fingerprint scanner (maybe excessive to have on the inside, but there was no such thing as being too paranoid in Parole), and pulled the door open without further question. "Yeah, come on in. What are you doing outside the library? I don't know if I've ever seen you not surrounded by books on all sides."

"True, this is a little, ah, out of my comfort zone," Rowan admitted, seeming relieved to be safely inside and out of the exposed corridor. They wore a floppy, oversized hat that only about half-hid their large, curling, ram-like horns, and a long skirt which concealed most of their goat-like legs, except for the very tips of their hooves. "But I figured this was important enough to risk it."

"What's important enough?" Jay headed back to his chair, sitting in a slightly more conventional way with only one leg slung up over the arm, in anticipation of diving back into what he did best. "Got someone you need me to feel out? SkEye automatons giving you a hard time?"

"No, nothing like that." Rowan's hooves clicked against the bare concrete floor as they came closer. "I just wanted to make sure you were all right."

"Me?" Jay looked up, surprised once more. Why was literally nothing today turning out the way he expected? But then, everybody had off days, even legendary cyber-revolutionaries. That still didn't make them suck any less. "Oh, yeah. Sure. Yes. I'm fine."

Rowan studied him with a skeptical, thoughtful gaze. Jay's greatest talents lay in electronic espionage, subterfuge executed from the safety of a small room with a screen and keyboard—not face-to-face. He had several tells, but one of the most obvious (which he realized almost immediately, internally kicking himself accordingly) was his tendency to answer uncomfortable questions very quickly, and around three times. That last one had been four.

"Okay," Rowan said with the patience of someone who knew exactly how much shit Jay was full of, but was determined to wade through it anyway. "But if you weren't—"

"Which I *am*."

"Just hypothetically," Rowan said with a slight raise of their hands. "Would there be something you'd want to talk about?"

"Hypothetically?" Jay leaned way back in his chair until he was staring at the ceiling, pushing himself back and forth with one foot against the desk edge. "I may have, theoretically, just... kissed Regan."

"Oh! Congratulations!" To their credit, Rowan didn't say 'it's about time' or any of the variations Jay was expecting, but their purely happy response told him they definitely weren't getting the point either. Which might have been a good thing. It meant he wouldn't have to explain what was really making him panic. "That's always a huge step. And nervewracking. But it went all right? I know he w—I mean, I'm sure he loved it."

"Yeah, and he was probably—actually, it's Regan," Jay amended with an anxious laugh. "I know he was just as nervous as I was, because he made this cute little surprised noise, like a squeak—never mind," he broke off, running a hand through his loose hair he was sure had been tied back with a scrunchie at some point today. No, nothing was going as planned. "He's just a ridiculously cute ace lizard-dragon-boy and I—I messed everything up, that's all."

"I'm sure you didn't. But if you want to tell me more about it..." Rowan's smile was slow, gentle, and entirely genuine. "I'm listening."

"It just kind of happened," Jay said, resting both hands behind his head and continuing to talk to the ceiling. "Like, I didn't even really think about it. It just seemed like the right thing to do, like, the *only* thing to do. So I did. And it was... *good*. Better than good. It was great, and not like, weird and dry and scaly at all, like you might think. His lips are soft, which I always figured they'd—I mean, it was nice, that's all. I haven't been, like. Pondering that. Or anything."

"It's fine if you have," Rowan said, and he could hear the smile in their voice without looking. "It's one of my favorite things to think about."

"Yeah..." Jay said faintly, only about three-quarters hearing whatever Rowan had just said, other, soft-lipped things on his mind. But when he finally came back to the here and now, his more-than-a-little loopy smile faded. "But that's not what..."

"What is it?"

"Right before that... I said I loved him." Jay shut his eyes tightly, sat up, and continued to lean forward until forehead met screen with a soft tingle of static. "And then I panicked. I didn't mean to say it, it was an accident. So when I said kissing him was the only thing to do, I meant it was either that, or try to take it back—which, I mean, *no?* Who does that?—or just bolt, just get outta there. And I couldn't leave *without* kissing him, because after that, I might... not... get..."

"You do love him," Rowan observed when he didn't finish the sentence. It was a completely accurate assessment, totally reasonable, and entirely unhelpful. "And of course you'll get another chance. Regan's not going to hold any of this against you; he understands panicking better than most people. It makes you do things you don't mean... but you did mean the important part."

"Yeah, but that's not..." Jay said again, then trailed off and made no effort to continue. For once, he'd lost the words.

Fortunately, Rowan found them. "You're thinking about him, aren't you?"

They took a few careful steps around Jay's chair, picking their way across the cluttered floor, until they had a better angle on both his face, and the framed Polaroid—a physical rarity for Jay's all-digital realm— photo hanging in a uniquely clean section of wall next to his workspace. A teenage Jay in a baggy band T-shirt and hair only down to his shoulders was sprawled across the lap of a slim, young South Indian man of about the same age. Both of their faces were lit up mid-laugh, eyes only for one another.

Jay didn't look up at Rowan or the photograph. Instead, he pulled his long legs back up and folded his arms around them, resting his forehead on his bony kneecaps that jutted through his torn jeans, shutting out the world. "Who else? Only the guy I think of, like, 25/8, whose short but incredible existence, and—and sacrifice, drives my every waking... whatever. Of course I'm thinking about him."

"You're driven by more than just him, Jay," Rowan said quietly. "There's more to your life than Mihir's death. But even so, what you're feeling is natural. It's normal, even if it's painful. Regan will understand that too."

Jay didn't answer immediately, looking up. When he did, his usually-lively voice was flat, almost a monotone. "The last time I told a guy I loved him, he died."

There was a beat of silence, interrupted only by the soft ambient hum of old computer fans, and the beeps of about a dozen urgent notifications, every one some crisis or another demanding attention he just didn't have it in himself to give.

"It wasn't your fault," Rowan said, voice still low, but inarguably firm. "Nobody could have done a thing, least of all you—"

"I know," Jay cut them off, looking up sharply. "My brain knows that, but my—my *fucking heart* doesn't, okay?" He fell silent, breathing surprisingly hard, as if he'd just sprinted a city block. "That never leaves this room, by the way, that I said that, or feel like... anything."

"Of course it doesn't," Rowan said without hesitation. "But you're not a machine, Jay. You just program them. Sometimes we get hurt, and there are no quick fixes."

"I know," he said, wryness coming back into his voice. It made a good cover for pain. "Every bug you fix, twelve more pop up. Everyone knows that."

"You know what I mean."

He did. Over the next few seconds, the sardonic smirk slipped off his face, leaving only exhaustion behind.

"I know that just because it happened once doesn't mean it'll happen again," Jay said at last. "But I can't help it. Saying it... it made it real. I do love him. And, yeah, the last guy I said that to, it didn't end well, that's all. And..."

Not for the first time, Jay's ever-present words fled from his head and his tongue as he let his eyes rest at last on the Polaroid photo. He didn't look right at it very often, eyes sliding automatically past it from one project to the other. It was like the sun, or what he remembered from before Parole. Necessary, life-giving, but painful to look at directly.

"The sun..." Jay mumbled, half-caught in the dream of that moment that was frozen forever on his wall. "That's what 'Mihir' means. I ever tell you that?"

"No, you didn't." Rowan's gentle voice brought him back to the present with a slight shock. Somehow, Jay hadn't quite expected an answer. "It's all right to talk about him, you know. We all miss him. Not in the way you do, but you're not alone in it. You never have been."

"Yeah..." Jay whispered, eyes still on the Polaroid, and the life he might have had if things had gone just a little differently. "I know. But I should be over it, that's all. Over him. It's been, what, four years? Isn't that long enough?"

"I don't think there is a 'long enough' when you lose someone like that," Rowan said simply. "Or even an 'over it.'"

"Oh," Jay said, eyes flicking over to Rowan now with a deadpan stare. "Great."

"I don't mean to say it'll never stop hurting," Rowan amended. "But it does—not so much get better, as *you* get better at handling it. You find ways. You invent your own. Someday, you realize that it's been an hour since it hurt last. Then, a little longer. Eventually... it's still there, but it doesn't paralyze you like it did once."

Jay didn't answer, and was struck by how often in this conversation he'd done that. Probably more than in the last year. Even when he was alone, he tended to talk to himself more. But he couldn't. All his words were just words, and sometimes words didn't even begin to be enough.

"Let me ask you this, Jay," Rowan continued, and Jay realized they'd probably spoken more in this conversation than in the last year too. Truly a red-letter day for both of them. "Do you think being with Regan is a betrayal, in any way?"

"No, it's not that," he said quietly. Somehow Rowan had a way of just asking point-blank questions that should have felt like a punch to the chest, but didn't. Jay hadn't been very glad to see them when they'd started talking. He was now. "I don't think he'd be mad, or feel left out or anything—he figured out about the same time I did that basically everybody we know is dating everybody in some way. Like even if he was alive now, I'm pretty sure he'd be fine. It just sucks that I can't... you know, ask him." He shifted again, stretching out his legs, feet flat on the floor. "I just—I don't want to get into anything and still be fucked up, you know? Regan deserves better than that."

"Do you think you're ready?" Rowan asked, and again, the directness and gentleness made Jay stop, think, and finally, find the words.

"I..." he paused, tried to be certain. Tried. "I think I am. I want to be. Regan makes me want to be. He makes me want to be better in a lot of ways. He makes me want to *get* better, too." He swiveled his chair to fully face Rowan. "What do you think?"

"It doesn't matter what I think," Rowan said quickly. "What's important is—"

"Yeah, yeah," Jay waved their protest away. "I know, you're trying to be all objective and crap, but guess what, that train left the station like, immediately—we're all way too freakin' close."

"It was worth a shot," Rowan said in a slightly ironic tone Jay thought sounded much more natural coming from himself. "But you're right."

"Sure am. So I'm asking you—knowing me, knowing Regan, and Mihir... what do *you* think, of any of this?"

Rowan was quiet for several seconds, and Jay dipped into an until-now-untapped well of patience to wait for an answer. "Only you can say if you're ready for this or not. Or if you and Regan are right for each other."

"I am," Jay said, more to himself than Rowan. "We are. I can feel it."

"And... I also think Mihir would want you to be happy. Whatever that means for you."

"Yeah," Jay said, surprised by the smile that spread across his own face. It was the certainty of hearing what he already suspected, the answer he already knew, just confirmed. Not quite permission, but it helped about as much. "Yeah—no!"

"What?" Rowan asked in startled response to Jay's sudden yelp.

"I just remembered—Regan's *already* happy without me! Because he's got Zilch, and—" Something even more relevant occurred to Jay, and he buried his face in his hands. "Aaghh! He's got *you!* And *I just spent like ten minutes whining to you about wanting to kiss your boyfriend!*"

"It's all right, Jay!" Rowan said, holding up their hands again and raising their voice only enough to be heard over his sudden panic flare. "I told you I was happy for you and I meant it. I'm happy for Regan too. I think you fit together very well already."

"Really?" Jay almost squeaked, peering up at Rowan through his fingers.

"Really. You're fine, and I'm truly glad you've gotten to this point. But ultimately, my opinion doesn't even matter here."

"I mean, it kinda does," Jay mumbled, resting his cheek on one fist and giving Rowan a tilt-headed look. "I'm not gonna date someone if his other datemate isn't cool with it. Or me. Oh jeez, that means I gotta talk to Zilch too..."

"I'm sure they'll be fine," Rowan said, giving a mildly dry look at the expression of growing terror on his face.

One thing Jay would never say, if he had a choice in the matter, was how off-putting he still found... the entirety of Zilch's existence. They were a nice person, really, and surprisingly chill—and intellectually he knew this. Instinct-wise, however, there was no part of him that did not want to scream and jump out a window seeing a person made of other dead people enter the room. He was working on it. At least Rowan was considerate enough not to comment.

"Not to speak for them," Rowan continued. " But the thing Zilch cares about most in this world is Regan being safe and happy. You make him both."

"Okay..." Jay said, trying to get a handle on his still-rapid breathing and heart rate. Fainting to escape a stressful situation, while occasionally tempting, was rarely productive. "Okay, that's good."

"Don't worry. We are very cool with it, and you," Rowan said with more calm and conviction than Jay felt he had ever expressed in his entire anxious, caffeinated life. "More than. There aren't many people I'd trust with Regan, to be honest."

"Oh," Jay said, feeling a faint warmth in his chest that was entirely, wonderfully different from a panic spike. "Thank you. That's big. Like, I know how big that is, and that's... wow."

"Mm-hmm." Rowan took a small step closer, reaching out to put one hand on his shoulder, steady and warm. "Really, Jay, the only person you need to talk to right now is Regan. He's not going to be mad at you— I feel like I know him well enough to say that much."

"Yeah. I know he'll be sweet about it. Wouldn't be so head-over-ass about him if he was the kind to, uh, not be. It's just that, believe it or not..." Jay said, looking up at Rowan with a sheepish, but slightly-less-terrified smile. "I'm not that great at talking about some things."

🔥

"Wow. That's a lot. You okay?" Ash asked after Regan was done telling him all about the nice—but stressful-sounding—thing that had just occurred, studying him with a watchful, concerned eye. "Because you can tell me if you're not."

"I'm fine," Regan said, and there was no shiver in his voice, or his spine, from the look of him. He really did seem about as serene as Ash had ever seen him, snuggled down into his favorite chair and its nest of blankets. Warmest, safest spot in the library. Maybe in Parole—safest, anyway; the rest of it was plenty warm. "But thanks for making sure."

"Of course," Ash said with a grin he hoped might help dispel any lingering anxiety Regan was still feeling but not showing. Regan was usually pretty easy to read, but you could never really know for sure. "Gotta check up on family. Dating Rowan means you're my little lizard-bro now."

"Step-bro?" Regan speculated.

"Bro-by-proxy," Ash smiled. "You're really okay? Because something like that would shock the hell out of me."

"I wasn't shocked, not really—I mean, the kiss was a surprise, but the first part wasn't. Jay's probably even more obvious about how he feels than me. He didn't really even need to tell me, but I'm glad he did." Regan nestled deeper into his blanket nest, like a dormouse settling in for a long winter's hibernation, safe and sound. "Jay can take his time. I'll be waiting for him when he's ready."

After he was satisfied that Regan was, in fact, fine, Ash stepped out of the room and into the hall where he'd almost collided with Jay, and now immediately almost collided with Rowan. They were in the middle of taking off a large, floppy hat Ash couldn't imagine actually fit over their horns, and stumbled back a few steps.

"Aahh, sorry," they said, but seemed distracted, ready to keep moving past Ash and into the room where everything was happening today, until they took notice of where Ash had just been. "Is he okay?"

"Regan?"

"Yeah." Rowan hesitated, and Ash recognized his sibling's distinctive look that meant they were weighing a great deal of information and wondering how much to ask or tell. People tended to confide in Rowan about things they'd never say to anyone else, and Rowan kept their mouth shut, never doing harm. Ash didn't push. The perks of being an older brother meant he usually found out anyway. "He tell you what happened?"

"He did, yeah," Ash said, unable to suppress a smile. "About time, really."

"Uh-huh. I just saw Jay." Rowan pointed behind them with their thumb. That explained the hasty going-out clothes. "He's a little shaken up, but he'll be okay."

"Regan too, I think," Ash said, cautiously optimistic. "He's handling it a lot better than I would, anyway."

"Good." Rowan was quiet for a moment, fidgeting with their hat and still seeming more restless than usual. Being out in public tended to do that to introverts—but sometimes it could have energizing effects too, going by their next suggestion. "Grab a bite?"

"Please," Ash said with a relieved sigh. Battling totalitarian police forces and sorting out friends and family's relationship hurdles were both exhausting but at least he was also pretty good at both. "Maybe a drink too. I don't even know what time it is, but I think the situation calls."

"It's always sundown when you haven't seen the sun in years," Rowan said, and Ash laughed. People generally had two reactions to the realities and oddities of life in Parole: cry or laugh. Ash knew which one he preferred.

"Right, right, no such thing as Parole time. Hey, speaking of, what day is it? You know, outside?"

Rowan gave a faint half-smile. "February 13th."

"Of course," Ash muttered as they left together. "Of course it is."

Knock-knock-knock.

"Password," Jay called in a guarded voice as he had the day before, holding perfectly still.

"Uh...your kung-fu is the best."

"I know, but what's the password?" Jay smiled as he undid the locks, even as his heart started to speed up. "Hang on, Regan."

"Hi," came Regan's voice in the empty-looking corridor, moments before the rest of him seemed to materialize on Jay's doorstep. "Thanks for letting me in."

"Hey, you knew the password." Jay said with an only slightly-nervous chuckle.

Regan curled up on the nearest blanket-covered surface, a chair that had once held the disemboweled remains of an ancient, boxy Macintosh, but now served a much more important purpose. It might not be as comfortable as a beanbag chair, but it belonged to Regan every bit as much.

Jay plopped back down in his swivel chair, turning back to a project he would probably have to do over, since he'd long since forgotten exactly what the end product was supposed to be. But that wasn't the point; fingers on keys and lines of code in front of his eyes was tactile, grounding, safe. It shrank the world to a manageable size, and reminded him that even if there were no quick fixes, sometimes there were still answers.

Regan stayed quiet too. He seemed comforted by the small, dark space and computer glow, and clack of the old-but-beloved keyboard. One reason of many he and Jay made such a natural fit.

A surprisingly comfortable silence stretched between them until Regan finally broke it, voice soft and tentative.

"So, about yesterday... are you doing okay?"

"Oh, yeah. Sure, yes." Jay said quickly, not breaking his typing rhythm. Damn, he'd done it again—but only three times. Maybe Regan wouldn't—

"Jay?"

"Hmm?" Of course he'd caught it. Of course he had.

"We don't have to talk about it."

"Oh, thank God!" Jay let out a whoosh of a sigh as the tension rushed out of him, practically melting into an exhausted puddle. "I'm so sorry for just dropping that on you and running—I didn't mean to—I just panicked," he stammered, desperate to explain. Why was it that as soon as Regan said they *didn't* have to talk about it, Jay found himself unable to do anything but that? "I didn't mean to say that even—I mean, that's not quite true. It was a good accident. I think. I just—fuck, I didn't want to change anything between us! But of course this changes things. You're just a really good thing in my life, Regan, that's all."

"You're one in mine too," Regan said. "One of my favorite good things. Some things will never change."

Like the way Rowan had of asking deeply personal questions without setting him on edge, Regan had a way of saying incredible things Jay would never believe coming from anyone else. Coming from Regan, he listened.

They were both quiet for a few seconds. As before, in the rare and special way that came from being with someone who truly understood him, Jay felt no need to fill the silence. When he finally did, it was with words he should have said a long time ago, or at least yesterday.

"I meant it, you know."

"I know," Regan said, with a little smile that made Jay's heart do a now-familiar, but always-thrilling jump. That hadn't changed either.

"I was just freaking out because…" Even before he'd stopped talking, Jay's eyes had begun to slide over toward the Polaroid on the wall. When he looked back at Regan, Jay saw him looking the same direction, expression bittersweet and fond.

"I know," Regan said again, more gently this time.

"It's been four years," Jay said faintly.

"So? You feel what you feel."

"Natural and normal, huh?" Jay said with a forced laugh that surprised him by turning real halfway through.

"As normal as anything gets in here." Regan's smile gradually became something else, something serious and solid. Like how Jay's asking-for-the-password voice was the spoken equivalent of a pokerface, Regan's expression was the facial version of a promise. "I'm here for whatever you're up for. Whatever it is, I'll be happy, because I'll be with you."

Jay couldn't answer at first. For a moment, it was enough to bask in that beautiful sentence, soaking in the warmth that was nothing like the fire beneath them, and everything like the sun they still saw in their dreams. Finally, he cleared his throat, and his mind, for the next step. "I, uh… there is actually something you could do for me."

"What's that?"

Jay took a slow, deep breath and let it out. Just as slowly, he rose to his feet and took another step—a physical one this time. "Kiss me again."

Regan stood up too. Closed the distance between them much more slowly and deliberately than Jay had the previous day. Jay's eyes slipped shut before Regan reached him, and he could feel his face flush and skin almost ache in anticipation. The wait had to only have been a split second but felt like much longer, an extended stay in the moment just after opening a door, just before stepping through it, the moment on the threshold, the nothing-and-everything hanging between.

Regan's lips met his for the second time in their lives, and it was like the first lungful of oxygen after waking from a dead sleep. Like before, it was soft and warm, the kind of touch he could melt into while the world stopped, secure as a thumbprint lock and reassuring as noisy keys. Unlike before, it was slow and sweet, with no desperation, no hesitation, and absolutely no question. Like grief and healing, this felt natural and normal as looking up to see the sun. Like they'd done it all their lives. Like there should never be a day without it, and now never needed to be.

When Regan pulled back and the world started turning again, it was just far enough for Jay to see the green lips he'd been so enjoying curl up into a smile. "I kind of forgot to tell you yesterday. I love you too."

Jay smiled back. Some words were worth the wait. "I know."

Life Returns

A ONE-SHOT FROM A TWITTER THREAD, OF ALL THINGS

The first thing Zilch does with their new hand is pull Rowan closer.

It's a quiet, subtle movement, in a city whose knife-sharp edges are defined by revolution. Parole's streets are filled with sweeping machinations, roaring infernos and heroic battles to save each new and fragile day. This is barely a shift of a thin wrist and two long, stitch-lined fingers, but in this room it's all that matters.

It always takes a while to get acquainted with a new limb. For the first day or so, connection is tenuous, sensation even more deadened than the rest of Zilch's reconstructed form. So they see more than feel

Rowan's fingers close around their new ones. The touch is dissociated, like the hand still belongs to someone else. With an unaccustomed flare of anxiety, they try to squeeze back, raise their arm—and fail. Suddenly Zilch feels every last stitch.

But they don't worry for long.

Rowan closes the distance between them, stroking the fine, lovingly meticulous stitches running across Zilch's face like they know each one, which they do, because Rowan put them there. This touch Zilch can feel. This warmth they remember long after their hollow chest has forgotten the feeling of a beating heart or lungs that breathe air.

Since their world began to change, Zilch has transformed dozens of times. Each time a risk, a renewal. Sometimes a full factory reset, leaving them unrecognizable. But every time, a change. A rebirth. But for every change, some things stay the same. With every reincarnation, there remain universal constants. Anchors. Zilch is loved, is alive, is not alone.

Rowan kisses them: deep, decisive, confirming. Everything else fades away. New arm, worn-down replacement parts, original skin, all are forgotten. Fire, empires, barriers, danger, all gone as well.

It's easy to lose hope in Parole. Or in yourself—or lose yourself entirely. But not everything stays lost. Sometimes you even find something new, precious, and real.

Zilch hasn't tasted much in years, but they swear they can taste sparks as they kiss back, holding on tight and one-handed and painfully aware of the rarity and fragility of their existence, unapologetic, all-promising and eternal. Rowan is soft and warm in their arms, and so, so alive, and the both of them are breathless, awakened, hearts and minds and lives fused like they've grasped a live wire together, carried on a shared magnetic, electric current.

They're certain. They both are.

Zilch has one arm wrapped tight around the small of Rowan's back. Like their better repair jobs, it fits as if it's always been there, and feels like it belongs. The other hand, newly born and not yet adjusted, moves almost on its own. Zilch's hand runs down a black horn's smooth curve, strokes Rowan's face, holds it as life slowly returns. Into their fingers, and into both of them, Neither of them even think about parting.

Live in this bleak, burning city long enough, and you'll start to feel life start to drain away. It takes moments like these, even brief and unplanned and quickly stolen, to get some of it back.

Sometimes Zilch thinks there might be an old life they miss. A barely-remembered, normal existence. A body that was their own, but never really felt like it. Even if Zilch's skin used to be whole and free of stitches, it never felt like it belonged to them. This feels like it belongs. They belong here, among curling horns and gleaming scales, and kisses as easy as breathing. Universal constants.

Some things will never change.

Happening Again

JUST UNDER A MONTH BEFORE CHAMELEON MOON
A FEW DAYS BEFORE THE LIBRARY GHOST

"I don't really see the point," Regan said, voice coming in loud and clear in Jay's earpiece. "That decision's kind of already made for me."

"Yeah, but is it the power you *want?*" Jay pressed, laying back in his reclining desk chair and staring at the ceiling.

His wall of monitors cast his dark apartment in a ghostly blue-green, but Regan's image wasn't on any of the many screens. A while ago he'd crossed into one of Parole's numerous dead zones, where even the almost-all-seeing CyborJ's video feeds couldn't reach, and when that

surefire recipe for an anxiety spike. Fortunately, audio contact tended to be easier to maintain. They probably had Radio Angel to thank for that. Never let it be said that Parole's undisputed technological champion didn't give credit where it was due.

"Given the choice of any ability in the world, anything at all," Jay continued. "You'd really pick being able to turn invisible? Again?"

"It's come in handy a few times…" There was a short silence and then a scuffling noise, like Regan was climbing something. There were a lot of fallen buildings in the area tonight's run had taken him, and probably even more hidden deathtraps. Jay wasn't overly concerned. Regan hadn't stayed alive this long by tripping and falling into pits. "Like every day."

"*Mrah*," said Seven, stretching up from the floor and headbutting Jay's hand. Most of the fluffy android cat's function during runtime was to be another monitor for Regan's vitals and general safety, alerting Jay of any danger. She seemed pretty calm for now, though, trying to get his attention just for petting, which he happily gave. She seemed to especially like being scratched on the exposed patches where Danae hadn't finished filling in her fur, which Jay appreciated. It felt like he'd made the right decision in bringing her home not-quite-finished. She was perfect the way she was.

"Okay, fine, invisibility is a good one for our, uh, current circumstances and living situation," Jay admitted. "But stop thinking about bare survival for a second, have some fun. You get to pick any superpower in the world, go, go-go-go."

"Do I still get to be a lizard?"

"Do you *like* being a lizard?" Jay asked as Seven jumped up onto his chair arm and started walking across it (and his chest) to the head rest.

There was a long pause, and Jay didn't break it. Regan might have been jumping between buildings, or going silent to avoid detection, or just thinking about his answer. Finally, one came. "Yes."

"Then you're a lizard for life," Jay declared, cracking his stiff knuckles. "But what else?"

"Um..." Regan hesitated, and the scuffling noise returned.

"This isn't distracting you, is it?" Jay asked a little more seriously. His eyes flicked over to where one of his illuminated screens displayed a set of numbers, monitoring Regan's heart, blood pressure, temperature, and other vital signs. The numbers were holding steady for now, but the program would alert him if any of them jumped. Seven didn't seem alarmed either, draping herself over Jay's head like a robotic cat hat. "If you need to focus, I'll put a sock in it."

"No, don't worry," Regan assured him. "I'm just trying to figure out how to get down from here. Looks like there's been a cave-in, landscapes changed. I think I'd want mind- reading."

"Oh, really?" Jay asked after the second it took for Regan's answer to sink in after the complete lack of segue. "Telepathy's cool, no doubt."

"Eh, maybe that's the wrong word," Regan said, sounding unconvinced of his own reasoning. "I don't think I'd want to know what everyone's literally thinking. Maybe just what they're feeling, so I know what they're planning before they do it. Like if they're actually dangerous or just scared or something."

"So more like being an empath. Betazoid, basically?"

Another pause. "*Star Trek?*"

"Aw, you do care. I'm touched, honestly." Jay chuckled, feeling genuine warmth in his chest under his casual lightness. Sometimes the little things in life really were the big things.

Regan made a flustered noise that wasn't quite words, and Jay stifled his laugh that threatened to grow. It was never a good idea for either of them to get distracted during runtime, but damn it, in Parole, you had to take your giggles where you could.

"So what would you pick?" Regan asked, sounding calm and collected again, but Jay could practically pinpoint the shade of vibrant green his frill would be now, the way it wiggled when he got flustered. Regan didn't exactly blush anymore, not in the way most people did, but he was never hard to read, especially not for Jay.

"Oh, that's easy. Five-second-rewind button." Jay folded his arms behind his head. Even though he'd been nearly lying on his back for the past half hour, he was only now starting to relax. Constant vigilance got exhausting after a few years. But right now, Seven was purring, Regan was doing well on a run, and they were having an enjoyable conversation that had nothing to do with hellish imprisonments or impending doom. This was as close to a perfect night as he could get—at least alone.

"Like time travel?" Regan asked, sounding a little confused.

"Yeah!" Jay smiled up at the dark ceiling; he could easily imagine the puzzled look on Regan's face, and enjoyed it almost as much as the thought of a rippling neck frill. "Do you know how many times I've said the exact wrong thing, then realized it like a millionth of a second later?"

"Um... a lot?" Regan teased, and now Jay laughed again.

"Babe, take whatever number you're thinking of and double it. I've stuck my foot in my mouth so many times I'm permanently tasting toe jam."

"Delicious," Regan said dryly. "Thank you for sharing that with me."

"I'm serious, though! I could go back until I said the right thing, or at least the thing that doesn't get everyone mad at me." Jay's smile turned sly. "Works for good things too though, not just mistakes. I mean, just picture it." He held up his hands, forming a lens-rectangle with his fingers and thumbs, and peered through at the dark ceiling. "I've got some SkEye creeps in my sights, they're *just* about to fall into one of my brilliant snares, and I just want to savor that moment, and watch them *eat it*, over and over again..."

"But why only five seconds?" Regan asked after another brief pause.

"Less chance of paradoxes," Jay explained readily, letting his arms flop back down to his sides. "Can't run the risk of accidentally becoming my own grandpa or something. Doesn't *remove* the possibility, obviously, but I figure there's less ways to shred the time-space continuum fabric in only five seconds—with infinite do-overs."

"You've put a lot of thought into this, haven't you?" Now Regan was suppressing a laugh, and Jay couldn't find it in himself to feel guilty for the distraction anymore.

"Hey, gotta do something to keep busy while you're out jumping off rooftops and stuff." A couple seconds of comfortable silence went by, and then Jay spoke again, voice dropping into something softer and rougher at the same time. "You know, I can think of something else I'd do with that five second rewind."

"What's that?" Regan asked, tone suggesting that he knew the answer and liked the idea just as much as Jay did.

"You're blushing right now, aren't you? The next time we're alone together, off the job, on the bed..." Jay let his eyes slip shut to better relish the image. "I'd wait until, uh, the opportune moment, and then totally see how many times I can make you—"

"Blush?" There it was, Regan actually giggled. Score, mission accomplished.

"Exactly." Jay grinned, basking in the satisfaction of knowing they were, as always, on the same page. He generally enjoyed their runtimes, but now he couldn't wait for this particular one to end. "Take whatever number you're thinking of, and then double it."

Silence.

Seven stood up quickly, one paw stepping on Jay's forehead. She wasn't alarm-meowing yet, but her fur did stand up a bit on end.

"Regan?" Nothing. Jay sat up, propping himself up on his elbows. "Regan, you good? I go too far there? Sorry, I know we're on a job and— oh, jeez, you're still into me ribbing you like that, sexy-wise, right?" He sat up the rest of the way and covered his face with his hands, wishing fervently for that five-second rewind right now. Regan had *sounded* into it, but that didn't mean he was, and going off the past eight years, he wasn't likely to say so if he wasn't. "I know it's kind of a flux, so if you're having a sex-neg day, you know you can tell me and I'll—"

"No, no, Jay, you're fine!" Regan answered at last, sounding breathless and so frightened it sent a cold stab of fear through Jay's stomach. "I'm just starting to think someone might be onto me after all."

"Mmrrrrrrrrr..." Seven started to let out an uneasy noise, then jumped from the chair to the desk, tail standing straight up and fluffed out. "Mrah!"

"Shit." Jay's feet hit the floor as he lurched upright and back to his work station just as the vitals screen started to flash a warning in reply to Seven's. Regan's heart rate and blood pressure had just spiked. So had Jay's, seeing that. "Somebody tailing you?"

"Yeah." Regan's voice was low and strained.

"Where?" Jay asked.

"Behind me, lights, radio chatter."

"Up or down?" Please say down, Jay begged silently. *Please* say down.

"Uh, up. I almost made it to the ground, but I'm starting to rethink that."

"*Shit!*" Jay shot an alarmed glance over at Seven, who was sitting expectantly by the main monitor, green eyes wide and fixed on him as if also requesting his help. "Okay, okay, sounds like they've got the high ground. But you've got something they don't."

"What's that?" Regan was breathing faster now and Jay could only hope it was from running and not panic. He'd see in a second.

"Me." Jay's fingers started to fly and multiple screen windows opened up. At first all they displayed was static—as he'd expected, Regan was still too far out for an actual visual— but with a keystroke, a grid-like overhead map of Parole appeared, one particular sector south of the center crater lit up yellow. "Okay, I've got your general position. You're still a little out of range for cameras, but I can scan for any—"

"*Jay!*" The sharpness of Regan's voice, a near-panicked cry, made him jump, and he froze in place for the space of a skipped heartbeat.

"Yeah?" he asked, back ramrod-straight now, hands anxiously hovering over the keys. "I'm right here!"

"*MrrrreeehH!*" Seven yowled, back arching in clearly distressed cat body language, staring right at the screen although Regan still didn't appear. She started to anxiously pace across the desk, back and forth.

"Here, Seven, this is down, down is good," Jay said absently, picking her up and dropping her on the floor at his feet. A moment later he felt her jump up onto the chair back, but didn't move her. She must be as scared as he was. "Regan, talk to me, what's happening?"

"*Jay it's...*" The rest of Regan's sentence dissolved into unintelligible static fuzz. "*...Found me!*"

"You're breaking up, babe," Jay said, voice tight as he struggled to clear up the rapidly deteriorating audio. "I'm boosting your signal as much as I can, just keep talking!"

"*Coming after... Bl... d in the... a—er—*"

Static blared through the earpiece, so loud and sudden Jay batted it off his head.

"Regan?" Nothing. Long seconds of horrible nothing, except for the static noise still pouring from the earpiece on the desk, and the screens Jay glanced back and forth between, as if either of them were actually helpful. "*Regan?*"

More nothing—until a piercing alarm beep made Jay jump again. He knew before looking that it was the vitals monitor, cold panic starting to seize his insides. But when he did look, he didn't see a flashing, sky-high heart and BP display like he'd feared. He didn't see anything. The numbers had reset to zero, as if nobody was hooked up to the monitors at all.

Nobody living, anyway.

Instead of freezing along with his blood, Jay felt shocked into action. The static finally clicked off as he picked up his fallen earpiece and switched it over to another frequency, sent out an urgent call request, and replaced it on his head with one shaking hand. His other hand kept typing, still fruitlessly trying to isolate Regan's now-nonexistent signature. Even the highlighted district had gone dark.

Finally, he let his hands drop to the desk, and, silent for once, waited for an answer. You never needed to announce yourself on this particular channel, which was good, because while some people glibly said Jay wouldn't shut up until the day he died—and maybe not even then—this brand of panic tended to knock every word right out of his head.

Jay gratefully noticed that Seven had stopped her anxious pacing, coming to rest again on the back of his chair. She'd started to purr, and the sound, specially tuned to anti- anxiety frequencies, calmed Jay down enough to let him think. He reached back to pet her soft, half-metal head as he gathered his scattered thoughts and tried to sort out something that wouldn't leave him alone.

Bl...d in the...a—er.

Jay mouthed the static-interrupted words, trying to complete the sentence. "A—er. In the a—er. Water? In the water. Bl..."

Blood in the water.

Oh.

For the third time, "*Shit.*"

"You've got Radio Angel," said a cheery voice in his ear and he jumped; he'd forgotten he was waiting on the line at all. If she'd heard his expression of rapidly escalating terror, she didn't give any indication. "Do I have the honor of talking to the illustrious CyborJ?"

"Yeah, uh—yeah, it's me," Jay managed to croak out, clearing his anxiety-thickening throat. "And we got a hell of a problem."

Regan's first coherent thought on regaining consciousness was *it's too bright.* He forced his eyes open to see a world out of focus, every direction a painfully intense white. The hot air was stale and biting at the same time, like the lingering smell of something burnt.

Ceiling, he realized. He was staring up at a bright white ceiling, lying down on his back on something hard and very cold. He tried to move, but something restrained his wrist—a metal cuff attached to the table on which he lay. More cuffs held down his other arm and both ankles. He was immobilized, and once he registered that reason to panic, he noticed another: his wrists and ankles were bare. His clothes were gone, and he was dressed in thin white paper like a disposable hospital gown. He shivered despite the room's unnatural heat, feeling vulnerable and much too exposed.

But it was the bright white light that scared him the most. He knew that light that came from all around him. He knew this room and everything that happened in rooms like it all over Parole. He was in a hot cell, a specialized room developed by SkEye for interrogations. The walls and floor were electrified, controlled by someone outside, and instantly ready to scorch anyone trapped within. Fortunately he wasn't on the floor, the one good part about being bound to a table. The dangerous floor wouldn't be able to touch him—at least not directly. He had the horrible feeling that he was still very much vulnerable to shocks. Metal was an excellent conductor.

And he wasn't alone.

"Don't bother asking where you are," said a harsh, drawling voice, and another surge of panic rose from Regan's stomach and swept down his spine in almost painful shivers. He knew that voice like he knew the room. It was slightly slurred, lisping as if the speaker's mouth was full. "You know what this room is. And you know who I am. Now look at me."

Heart pounding so hard it hurt, Regan forced his aching eyes into focus and turned his head, searching for the source and praying every second he was wrong.

He must have taken too long, because something slammed into the table that felt like a frustrated kick, jarring Regan painfully and making him gasp. "I said *look at me.*"

Finally, Regan saw him; the last person he'd ever wanted to see again in his life. The man who stood beside Regan's metal table was an unusual one for Parole, in the sense that there was very little remarkable about him. White, early forties, average height and build, short brown hair, nondescript face. So ordinary he was almost forgettable—except for when he smiled, Regan thought with a stab of nausea. He wasn't smiling yet, but Regan anticipated it like waiting for a blow.

"Sharpe," Regan whispered, stomach lurching.

"Hello, Chimera." His light blue eyes traveled up and down Regan's entire restrained body—and now he smiled, and everything mundane about him quickly turned to horror. His teeth were like a shark's: huge, wickedly pointed, protruding slightly. Too big to easily fit in a human mouth, hence the somewhat garbled speech. Regan understood that to some degree. It had taken him a long time to learn how to talk with a too-long tongue, and he retained a slight lisp he'd never be able to shake. But that was all he'd ever understand about Sharpe, and all he'd ever want to.

"You know, Turret's been after you for a long time," said the SkEye lieutenant, pointedly flashing as many teeth as possible with every word. He started to lazily pace in a circle around the table, and Regan lost sight of him as he passed behind. "He'll be so glad to see you're back. How long's it been? Eight years since the rogue agents Chimera and Zero up and disappeared? But you'd know all about disappearing, wouldn't you?"

Regan couldn't speak. He held perfectly still, as if he could indeed hide in plain view. The awful part was that Sharpe was right, he could turn invisible whenever he wanted, but it wouldn't do any good now, restrained. It would be a waste of energy, and he had the feeling he'd need every bit to survive whatever came next.

"You disobeyed orders," Sharpe said, lowering his voice as he came back into view, continuing his slow circumnavigation toward Regan's feet. "You and Zero both. Got it into your head that you had a choice in any of this, and then you ran."

Regan's eyes flicked around the room, looking frantically for a way out, but he knew it was futile. Hot cells were secure, almost impossible to escape even if he weren't tied down. He was dead already, he knew. Sharpe would absolutely kill him... but not right away.

"But now you're back," Sharpe continued, ever self-congratulatory, ever appreciative of the sound of his own voice, and the opportunity to expound before a quite literally captive audience. Right now, Sharpe spoke casually, as if they were discussing plans for a fun day out, but Regan was well acquainted with the way he could turn, vicious and deadly all at once. "With me. And you're going to tell me all about Parole's resistance. Starting with the slippery CyborJ."

Regan said nothing. His voice would shake and crack if he tried. But the fact that Sharpe was asking this at all meant Jay was safe—he hadn't been able to track CyborJ's signal. The moment Regan had known he was about to be captured, he'd ripped his earpiece and vitals monitor off, stomped them to pieces, and flung the remains off the rooftop. Now the pieces were scattered along some alley floor, useless to everyone, but especially Sharpe.

"And you're not going to want to tell me, of course." Sharpe was behind his head again. Regan shivered. "We both know how this goes—but it'll still be fun. And by the time I'm done, you'll be a new man."

As terrifying as looking at Sharpe was, it was so much worse when Regan couldn't see what he was doing, when he never knew where he'd come from next. It made his panic rise again, made him redouble his efforts to break free, hard metal cutting painfully into his wrists.

"I wouldn't do that if I were you," Sharpe said as his latest circuit brought him back into view. "Turret told me to bring you in alive—check. And unharmed. Also check—for now. And to make sure you were functional and useful—and compliant—by the time he got here. Which you will be... but he didn't tell me not to have fun in other ways."

Sharpe grinned, a horrible smile Regan had seen too many times in his dreams, and would continue to see whenever he closed his eyes, assuming he lived long enough. For the first time, Regan noticed he held something in one hand, something he couldn't quite see, or at least consciously identify. Before he got a good look, Sharpe was behind him and gone again.

"I am going to make you scream," Sharpe grated suddenly, directly in Regan's ear. The shock made him jump and struggle against the restraints, made a cold chill sweep through him, and he knew if he looked down he'd see his body starting to turn invisible despite himself.

"I am going to make you beg for me to stop. So many times."

Fear washed over Regan's entire body like a wave, a panic so overwhelming his skin began to sting. He could feel Sharpe's hot breath on his cheek, ear, loose frill of skin on his neck, which shivered like a leaf in a hurricane. His breath smelled sharp as his teeth, and metallic, a primal smell that sent every one of Regan's survival instincts raging for escape.

Blood in the water.

"Take whatever number you're thinking of..." Sharpe whispered. "And then double it."

Jay. Sharpe heard. Sharpe heard them. He knew, he knew, he knew—

"No—" Regan's terrified cry cut off in a gasp.

Because now Sharpe brought his hand up again, revealing what was inside. A syringe, filled with a bright green fluid shining in the too-bright light, maybe giving off its own. In a movement like a cobra's strike, Sharpe plunged the tip into Regan's exposed upper thigh and pressed the plunger down.

Regan barely had time to scream, or register the pain, as the needle went in. A rushing noise filled his head, and a surge of heat flooded from the needle prick through his entire body. The wicked current was so intense it felt like the hot cell's electrified floor had come to life after all.

But at the same time, his senses erupted into a strange euphoria. Pleasure mingled with the pain as his every cell felt energized to the point of exploding into starbursts. It felt like drowning and lungs filling with air at the same time. It felt like coming alive and dying, like being filled with a power no human body was meant to withstand, and knowing that even if he did, nothing would ever be the same.

Blood pounded in his ears, and Regan lost himself in the noise. The last thing he saw were teeth, inescapably close and terminally sharp.

"So that's everything Jay told me," Radio Angel said, voice transmitted into three new earpieces on a secured frequency. She spoke fast, filling the new runners in on the situation as quickly and efficiently as possible. Most of the time, she was a bouncy ball of sunshine, but even she knew when to get serious. "Is that enough to go on?"

"It'll have to be," said Ash, usually cheerful voice grim. "We'll head to his last coordinates, obviously, and split up once we get... okay, I guess we're already splitting up."

"Zilch go off on their own?" Radio Angel guessed, unsurprised. Zilch had to be terrified, and they'd be an unstoppable juggernaut until Regan was safe.

"Yep. Guess it's me and Celeste for now—since I finally convinced Annie to sit this one out. We're heading out."

"Gotcha." She paused, but had never been able to maintain radio silence for long, especially when she was worried about her friends. And now, with each minute that passed, their chance of finding Regan before someone else did diminished. "How's Jay? He sounded pretty rattled."

"Yeah, because..." Ash stopped and paused for a moment. "It's probably best not to speculate. We're just going to find Regan before anything else happens, that's all."

"Okay," she said. "Good luck, I'll be here if you need me."

"Always are. Going dark now."

Once his voice faded, Radio Angel switched over to a new frequency, one more private than the group call.

"Celeste?" she asked, nervousness creeping into her voice now that they were one-on- one. Radio Angel—Kari—had never needed masks when talking to her. "You haven't said a word all night. You doing okay?"

"I just don't like losing people," came Celeste's clear, clipped tones. Kari knew her voice well enough to know Celeste was covering something up, probably worry. "Especially not if we're really dealing with..."

"With what?" Kari pressed gently. "I knew Jay wasn't giving me the whole story, and Ash is totally hiding something too. You know you don't have to do that with me. What's got you all so worried?"

Celeste didn't answer right away. When she did, her voice was so hard and steely it gave Kari the shivers. "We're just going to find him, that's all."

🔥

For what felt like forever, Regan didn't know his own name.

He didn't know how long he'd been here, lost in electric currents and a scalding undertow that destroyed and rebuilt him by the second, every inch of him caught between screaming agony and soaring ecstasy. Hours, days, weeks, or maybe just a few frantic, spinning breaths, interrupted by needles and shocks. But where he'd once felt like he was drowning, now he floated, easy and serene, buoyed on a slow current that carried him from darkness into light so brilliant he thought maybe for the first time in almost a decade, he could see and feel the rays of the sun Parole had almost forgotten.

But, just like the sun, all good things were gone too soon. Without ceremony or warning, Regan found himself back in a body where everything hurt, hot and shivering at the same time, wanting to contract and curl himself into a ball, but restrained by sharp metal digging into his wrists and ankles.

He didn't want to open his eyes. He couldn't remember where he was, but knew nothing good would greet them, not with the sharp, burnt-antiseptic smell and too-bright light already assaulting his senses and the cloying, metallic scent he knew too well to mistake. And not with the lingering aftershocks of pleasure tingling through his veins, strange and incongruous and entirely unwelcome.

That was Parole's worst-kept secret, and most damning truth. Chryesdrine felt good. Regan didn't *want* it to feel good. He didn't want to enjoy the knowledge that *he was infected again*, he'd been re-dosed, knew right now that he was re-addicted even if the pangs had yet to set in. They would, and all too soon, he knew it as surely as he knew Parole's fire still burned beneath him. *It would be easier if it didn't feel good,* he thought with a gasp that nearly became a sob. It would be better if the drug only brought pain, then he could hate it in peace, and not feel like his body itself was betraying him even as he despaired.

He dragged his eyes open and waited for the painful landscape to resolve itself. When it did, again he saw teeth, just as close and deadly as when the needle had punctured his skin and sent him falling into a mind-obliterating, scalding, euphoric sea.

"There, now. That's better," Sharpe said, voice low and sickeningly satisfied. "Nice and cooperative."

Terror surged through Regan like another injection burning through his veins, but this one carried no pleasure at all. Every inch of his skin stung, and the panic-pain wasn't only skin deep; he burned down to his bones, and he didn't know if it was aftershocks from the hot cell's cruel currents, or Chrysedrine's addictive poison taking hold of him from the veins out. He strained at the shackles but only succeeded at slicing into his wrists so hard he was sure he'd draw blood long before he escaped.

"Spoke too soon," Sharpe amended, sounding disappointed, and sat back a little, folding his arms. He'd brought a folding chair in here, sitting opposite Regan's table. How long had he been watching and waiting? "Go ahead, tire yourself out. Yesterday was fun. I'm up for some more, and I can go all night."

Yesterday...? But Regan couldn't have answered if he'd wanted to. His mouth didn't work, and words wouldn't connect in his exhausted, scorched brain. All he could do was tear his eyes away from Sharpe's grinning face and glance one more time around the hot cell, scouring the harsh white light for something, anything that would help him—

Someone appeared in the corner behind Sharpe. Not through a door or window, but seemingly from thin air, without sound or warning.

A young man, or maybe a teenager, floated several feet in the air, which seemed to deteriorate around him somehow, almost like a grainy old film recording with dust and scratches flashing across a washed-out image on a screen. The boy himself didn't fit with the rest of the room, aside from having appeared from nowhere. He was strangely... colorless, Regan thought. Almost like sepia, even more like an old movie, which contrasted starkly with his black skinny jeans and Converse sneakers, and long, unruly white hair that seemed to blow in a breeze Regan didn't feel at all. But the strange figure didn't just lack color, but solidity. Maybe it was a trick of the light—maybe all of this was a trick of his tortured brain —but Regan was sure he could see through the newcomer like a thin curtain. Like a ghost.

Regan was just about to write it off as a hallucination, Chrysedrine infecting his mind like a virus and making him see things that weren't real as well as feel them, when the ghost boy's face lit up in a smile, as if he recognized Regan like an old friend. Looking nearly as smug as Sharpe, but nowhere as predatory, he raised one hand in a cheery wave.

"Who are you?" Regan whispered, staring in spite of himself. He'd seen things that weren't there before, but they'd always been places and people he knew. This place, and this man in the chair, almost always. His brain had never conjured up an entirely new person before, but there was a first time for everything.

"Really?" Sharpe chuckled, a sound that sent a new wave of shivers cascading down Regan's aching spine. "Thought we'd been over this last round. You need me to show you who I am again? Fine by me. It never gets old."

But, for the first time, Regan wasn't paying attention to him. He stared, transfixed, as the ghostly young man drifted down from his spot near the ceiling to float directly over Sharpe's shoulder.

"Hi there," he said, remarkably casually for someone in a hot cell, even if he wasn't the one in the hot seat, and possibly not there at all. "Call me Hans."

"Are you... really here?" Regan rasped, his sandpaper-rough throat aching for water. However long he'd been in here, he hadn't had a drink, that was for sure.

"Oh, I'm here," Sharpe said with an unwholesome leer, sitting up and leaning forward to rest his elbows on his knees.

"Ehhh, kinda," said the ghost boy at the same time, speaking over Sharpe as if he wasn't there. He gave a see-saw motion of one semi-transparent hand. "Long story. Better question is, do *you* want to be here?"

"No," Regan whispered, eyes wide and unblinking. Could this really be happening? Parole was home to all sorts of people with incredible abilities. Had one of them actually come to rescue him? A stranger who really was a new friend he hadn't met yet?

"No?" Sharpe repeated softly, dangerously, raising his eyebrows and staring in a way that made Regan's stomach twist despite his newfound hope. "Is that what you said?"

Regan hesitated. Sharpe didn't seem to be able to see or hear the boy who called himself Hans, and if Hans could see him, he was ignoring him right back. Both of them were giving Regan their undivided attention, and nothing made him want to run and hide quite like the spotlight.

"So, you're asking me to save you, is that it?" Hans asked, still unnervingly casually, as if they weren't in a SkEye detention center, Regan wasn't wearing shackles and a singed paper gown that looked out of place against his unburned skin, and Sharpe wasn't here at all.

"Yes," Regan whispered desperately. If this was a hallucination, it was the most promising one he'd had yet. "Yes! Save me!"

"Save you?" Sharpe grinned, seemed almost about to break into the laugh that haunted too many of Regan's dreams, but then seemed to notice Regan wasn't looking at him, but past him. Frowning, he turned in his chair to look behind him—directly at Hans. But he didn't react, not so much as a start or tensing of his shoulders. When he looked back at Regan he simply looked bemused. It wasn't an expression Regan associated with him, and he almost laughed. "Maybe we gave you a little much in that last shot. You should be nice and lucid by now..."

Hans smirked, cocked his head, and stuck one fist on his hip, looking every bit as if he'd just won a very high-stakes bet. "Your wish is my command."

He snapped his fingers, and with that, he was gone, as if he'd never been there. The air cleared in his absence, and silence returned. Once more, Regan was alone with Sharpe.

"Well, never mind. Now that you're paying attention I can tell you this," Sharpe said, and Regan's eyes followed him as he slowly rose from his chair. Now that all Regan had to focus on was his captor, all the fragile hope he'd allowed himself crumbled in an instant. He was right back where he started: weak, restrained, half-naked, and painfully afraid. "I'm so glad you're back, Chimera. The place just hasn't been the same without you."

Regan shuddered, a long, violent tremor that shook him to his core. For the first time, he directed his laborious words toward Sharpe. "Don't. Call me that."

"Call you what?" Sharpe scoffed. "Your name? The one you got when you signed up to join us—entirely by choice, if you'll recall."

"Wasn't a choice," Regan shot back with a flare of unwise but inarguable fury. Maybe speaking to Sharpe was a loss, playing into his hands, but Regan was past caring. "Not if death's the only alternative."

"Given the option of an extraordinary life over any kind of death, I know what I'd pick every time," Sharpe said, grinning so widely Regan could almost count every too-pointed tooth. "And I think you would too. You were good at your job, Chimera. We were lucky to have you — and you're lucky to be back where you belong."

He stepped toward Regan, but instead of circling as he had before, he reached out to pull back the paper gown, exposing Regan's thigh where he'd plunged the Chrysedrine syringe. Regan tried to shrink away from his too-rough fingers, but of course couldn't move, and couldn't keep from staring at the nausea-inducing sight of Sharpe's hand on his skin. But even that was strange. What Regan could see of his own flesh was his equivalent of pale, a sickly gray-green. But by Sharpe's hand, where the needle had punctured him, his skin was a vibrant emerald, even brighter, more intense than it usually was. It somehow looked more robust, a center of healing that bled off again too soon into sickness.

"Look, you're not hurt anywhere," Sharpe said, words full of false comfort and a too true threat. "Couple sessions in a hot cell and you're good as new. That means the Chrysedrine's working its magic. And didn't it feel good?" He let out an awful chuckle as Regan shuddered and clenched his teeth so tight his head started to ache. "Never mind. I know it was good for you. So now, we can pick up right where we left o—"

"*Sir?*" A voice crackled through some invisible speaker, confirming what Regan already knew from experience. The room was being surveilled, probably with hidden cameras as well as recording devices. But this man's voice sounded anxious, not impassive and cold as he remembered SkEye interrogations. "*We've got a problem.*"

"What is it?" Sharpe snarled, but didn't look away from Regan, or move his hand.

"*Systems are going haywire,*" said the man on the speaker, sounding increasingly confused. Against his will and better judgement, Regan empathized. "*Like nothing we've ever seen, it's like—it's like something's physically tearing our hardware apart from the inside!*"

Now Sharpe released his hold on Regan's thigh, and Regan almost had time to rejoice, hyperaware and dizzyingly grateful for the absence of the most unwelcome touch—but it was only to lurch forward, leaning in much too close to Regan's face. Now Regan squeezed his eyes shut, but he could still smell Sharpe's breath, foul and unmistakably bloody smell stinging the insides of his nostrils like the worst of Parole's toxic smoke.

When Sharpe spoke, his voice was just as inescapable, a harsh and grating sound that would force its way into Regan's head for weeks to come, if not longer. "I'll be back before you know it."

Regan heard a sharp clatter of metal, as if Sharpe had kicked over his chair. Then footsteps, followed by the sound of the cell's disguised door sliding open and shut. Then nothing.

Until a new and different laugh filled his ears. Regan opened his eyes to see Hans floating before him again, both hands on his hips this time, like a slightly older Peter Pan, but more modern, more ghostly, and just-as-devilish.

"What did you do?" Regan gaped, every bit as surprised to see him back as anything else that had just happened.

"Nothin'," Hans grinned, and gave a bouncy shrug of his thin shoulders. "Let's see if I can do it again."

With that, he reached one clearly non-corporeal hand into the head of Regan's metal table, where it disappeared completely. Its restraints must have been computerized too, because the cuff on his right wrist immediately snapped open. Regan barely had time to gasp before the rest followed, one right after the other.

But being released wasn't the same as being free. Before he could gather his fuzzy senses and questionable strength nearly enough to climb down, Regan found himself falling, unrestrained but unsupported, and crumpling to the hot floor. He lay there in a curled heap as he struggled to catch his breath, not at all sure his limbs would support him, or that he wouldn't pass out again immediately upon finding his feet.

"Come on!" Hans urged, tilting in the air like he was swimming, 'diving' until his face hovered just a foot or so above Regan's. "I got you a chance to escape, but you're the one who has to take it!"

"Why are you helping me?" Regan asked, still weak and shaking on the floor, trembling with the strange pleasure left over from Chrysedrine's violent, cell-deep overhaul. He couldn't stand. And, even now, couldn't trust. Nobody helped for nothing. Not here. Not in Parole, and especially not in a detention center under the watchful gaze of its deadly Eye in the Sky.

"Are you kidding?" Hans retorted. "We can talk about the why later! You gotta move! Now, now, now, before Sharpe catches you again!"

Regan couldn't argue with that. Or begin to guess who Hans was, how he got here, how he knew Sharpe's name, how he knew Regan was here at all. But Hans was right about one thing. Sharpe would come back. He always did. But when he did, Regan wouldn't be here.

Summoning every bit of strength, and praying for Chrysedrine's wonderful, terrible blessing to last at least until he was safe, Regan pulled himself to his feet and staggered from the room.

Real sunlight in Parole was almost as rare as water. While the sides of the energetic barrier were clear enough to see through toward the ground, as the dome rose, it grew opaque, blocking out most of the sun, and all the stars and moon. The strongest light source came from below, from the fires burning under the pavement and sometimes creeping up through the cracks. Today, the sunset of the second day since Regan had disappeared, the eerie orange light seemed even less comforting.

"You know, right before all this happened, Regan and I were talking about—this is so dumb," Jay said, running his hands down his face. He'd been doing that more and more frequently every hour he'd gone without sleep, and both he and Rowan had lost count by this point. "What superpowers we'd want if we got to pick. And I said I'd want to be able to zip back in time five seconds to do things over. And now... all that's playing in my head is those five seconds, right between everything being fine, great, and then realizing something was wrong. Over and over. Be careful what you wish for, right?"

"There's nothing you could have done, Jay," Rowan said, so gently and with such certainty Jay almost believed them.

"Yeah, tell that to the loop my brain's stuck in."

They sat together in the back room of the library, one of the most secure places in the building, and therefore, most of Parole. Regan's beanbag and blanket nest sat between them, conspicuously empty. On the book-covered desk also sat a pair of the only kind of phones that worked in Parole, ancient, disposable burners, specially rigged to work on Jay's home-brewed cellular signals. They hadn't rung in a while, but both Rowan and Jay kept stealing glances at them as if the next call would be from Regan saying he was on his way home.

"You're thinking about him again, aren't you?" Rowan asked, breaking the exhausted silence that had fallen between them.

"Regan?"

"No," Rowan said. They didn't need to elaborate, and Jay didn't need to ask.

"Is it that obvious?" Jay dragged a hand down his face again, then simply rested his forehead in his palm, eyes shut. The past two days felt like a physical weight pressing down on his shoulders. The only thing that came close was the weight of the past ten years. Gradually, that had eased until he could go weeks without feeling it, days without even thinking about it, and then feel guilty for forgetting. "Just feels like it's happening again, that's all."

"It's not," Rowan assured him, and even though their voice didn't shake or sound remotely unsure, he still had to wonder if the reassurance was meant for him alone. "We'll get him back. He's not Mihir—and neither one was your fault."

"I know," Jay mumbled. "Or my brain does at least. Took it long enough. Still nice to hear it sometimes though, thanks." He squeezed his eyes shut a little tighter and pressed the heels of his hands against them, watching the firework pinpricks appearing from the darkness. "God, I just can't stop thinking about it. Regan. His vitals going dark, losing his signal, and what he said right bef..." he stopped talking. Stopped rubbing his eyes too. Held very still.

"What did he say?" Rowan asked, sounding puzzled.

"Nothing," Jay said, a little too quickly. He didn't uncover his face or look up. If he looked up, it made lying to Rowan ten times harder than it already was. Still, it was better than the alternative. "Forget I said anything."

"No, really, what did he say?" Rowan peered at Jay curiously, and obviously aware by now that he was backpedaling fast. "It might be important."

"Seriously, it's nothing, it's fine, you don't have to worry about it." Damn. Four denials. Not good for maintaining a facade of calm believability. Even the best of Jay's lies tended to fall apart around three.

Thankfully, Rowan didn't pursue the obvious smokescreen. Instead they gave a little laugh that turned into a sigh. "Worrying is about all I'm good for right—"

Brrrrt. The sound of a vibrating phone startled them both into silence, and they turned to see Jay's lighting up. He almost knocked it onto the floor in his rush to grab it up and answer.

"That you, Z?"

"It's me," came Zilch's voice. They sounded even flatter on the phone, or maybe it was just their state of mind. They had to be sick about this. "Still nothing out here. Has he called home?"

"You'd be the first to know," Jay said. "Well, third, I guess."

"Zilch?" Rowan cut in suddenly, sharp anxiety in their voice making Jay shut his mouth and look up immediately. They were on the edge of their seat and leaning forward, entire body looking tense as if they'd come close to jumping right out of their chair. "It's Sharpe, isn't it? He's the one who has Regan, isn't he?"

There was a long pause while Jay's heart and stomach seemed to drop through the floor and Rowan froze, as perfectly still as Jay had been the second he realized he'd said too much.

"We're doing everything we can," Zilch said at last. "And we're going to find him."

"That's not an answer, Zilch." Rowan's voice took on a brittle-sounding urgency Jay rarely heard in it. "Please, if Sharpe is involved, I need to know."

Another long pause. Jay wanted to be anywhere else, think about anything else, but couldn't bring himself to move or speak. Neither did Rowan. But when Zilch finally did, they spoke without pretense or excuse.

"We think Sharpe is involved, yes," they said, the plainness of their words almost surreal. Zilch wasn't nearly as emotionless as people tended to think, Jay knew, far from it, but right now, nobody would ever know. "The last we heard from him was 'blood in the water.' But *we're not giving up*," they emphasized as Rowan audibly gasped. "Blood in the water doesn't mean he's not coming home. And Rowan..."

"Yes?" Rowan leaned a little further forward, clearly hanging on whatever Zilch would say next, as if it was the only thing that mattered. The only thing in the world.

"We'll get him back. He's coming home. I'll make it happen."

Rowan let out the breath they'd obviously been holding, and some of the painful-looking tension left their shoulders. "I know you will."

"Sorry," Jay said as he hung up, rubbing his aching eyes again and still unable to meet Rowan's. "How'd you know?"

"What's the single worst thing that could possibly be happening to Regan right now?" Rowan didn't sound angry, exactly, which is what Jay would have preferred. But they did sound distressed and several degrees more scared than before. "That both you and Zilch would try to hide—why wouldn't you tell me? Sharpe might have him! Regan as much as said so, and you and Zilch—"

"I know! I'm sorry!" Jay said again, more desperately this time. "I wasn't trying to keep it from you, really! I just—I couldn't tell you or Annie that—"

"Well, of course not Annie!" Rowan said, undisguised frustration entering their voice for the first time. "But I'm not a teenager, Jay, you and Zilch don't have to protect me, and this is *exactly* the kind of thing I need to know about, so I can do my job!"

"I know!" Jay stuck his face in his hands again, as if that would make everything stop falling apart. "I just couldn't—I didn't want to say it. Not until we knew for sure. Saying it to anyone who didn't know, out loud, it would just mean it's really happening, and if there was a chance it wasn't, I just... wanted..."

He trailed off, unable to find the words to explain something he didn't fully understand himself. Rowan broke the silence not with words, but the sound of a chair sliding back and their hooves against the hardwood floor. Jay looked up at last to see them almost to the door.

"Where are you going?" he asked, suddenly finding the thought of being left alone in the room Regan slept in almost as awful as it being unoccupied entirely.

"I'm going to get a room and some supplies ready for when Regan gets back. If it really is Sharpe, he'll be in bad shape," Rowan said, opening the door but not yet stepping through it. They half-turned back to face Jay, shoulders sagging. Until now, Rowan hadn't given the impression of being particularly stressed or fatigued, but now they looked every bit as exhausted as Jay felt, and just as scared. "I'm sorry for snapping at you, Jay. I understand why you didn't tell me—I don't want to think about it either. But now I know what to do to give Regan the best chance of getting through this."

"Okay," Jay said quietly, feeling a fraction less devastated. Maybe he hadn't screwed everything up beyond all recognition yet, at least not with Rowan. "Uh, can I help?"

"Please. I have a feeling I'll need another pair of hands." Something that wasn't quite a smile, but at least eased some of their obvious distress, crossed Rowan's face. "And thank you. It's just better to not be alone."

Hans had a plan. Of sorts. Fortunately, everything so far seemed to be going according to it. He'd distracted Sharpe, freed the prisoner from under his nose, and now if all continued to go well, they'd be out of here soon. And so far, Hans was doing a pretty good job of making it seem like he had much more of a plan than he actually did.

He'd known the moment he saw Regan in the library just a few days ago. This was the man he needed, the one who would help Hans achieve everything he'd worked and waited for, for so long, whether he wanted to or not. But it wasn't just a short glimpse in the library that told him so. He'd remembered, once he had time. A man with green skin had almost—*almost*—been the one to free him from a detention center even more secure than this one, eight years ago. Now Hans was returning the favor, and then some. Regan wouldn't *almost* do anything by the time he was done.

"Who are you?" Regan asked suddenly, after they'd made a few turns down the thankfully deserted hallway. He'd been following where Hans led him so far, but now he was starting to question. Hopefully not too much.

"I told you, I'm Hans."

"Do I... know you?" Damn, he was definitely getting closer to asking the right questions. But still, the poor guy looked so confused. And hurt and tired and very small, so much smaller than Hans would expect from someone who'd given SkEye so many headaches over the years.

"Ha, nope." Hans lied, and laughed a little, but it wasn't a happy one. His laughter hadn't been genuinely happy for... he couldn't remember. Longer than he'd been a ghost. "Nobody knows me."

Regan didn't seem to know what to make of that. He had to still be woozy from the Chrysedrine; going by the number of injections Sharpe had given him, that would last a while. Then, of course, would come withdrawal. But in between he'd have a few hours of relative functionality—probably actually enhanced, stronger and faster than he would have been before the injection. They had to use that.

"Do you know *me?*" Regan asked, peering around the next corner. He seemed to be recovering from his weakness in the interrogation room, moving with greater ease and complete silence, but still wasn't able to go completely invisible—or what counted for invisible to anyone who wasn't Hans. Hans didn't have physical eyes to fool.

"I know *of* you," Hans said, and that much was true, if not the whole truth. "You're kind of an urban legend. Like alligators in the sewers. Except this big lizard can disappear into thin air, and knows how to kill people in a whole lot of interesting ways."

"What?" Regan stopped, eyes going wide. He looked so scandalized Hans almost laughed. "I don't know who you think I am, but—"

"I think we better keep moving," Hans said, and continued down the hall until Regan followed without further argument. He kept moving, hoping to avoid any more questions, and it seemed to work, until they reached the door Hans wanted. He stopped, and so did Regan, but he didn't look happy about it.

"Why are we stopping?"

"Because this is the security office," Hans said, wondering if he was about to have to improvise a way to convince Regan to walk through that door now that they'd finally reached it. Seemed to be a new problem every step of the way.

"I know what it is," Regan said, shying away from it. "That's *his* office."

"Yeah," Hans replied, telling himself that the stab of anxiety he felt was impatience and not a very real and shared knowledge that 'his office' was never a place anyone went voluntarily. "Sharpe's got what we need to get out of here."

"Going in there's a bad idea," Regan said, shaking his head and taking a step backwards. He was completely right, and if Hans had a body, he'd have been taking that same step—but if Hans had a body, he wouldn't be in this mess at all. "Really bad. We could get trapped in there. We should keep looking for a way out."

"We could, but there's about twenty guys between us and the only exits," Hans said, trying to sound casual despite his growing unease. It wasn't that he was overly concerned with getting trapped, walls hadn't been able to hold him in years. But Regan kept saying 'we, us,' like he was counting Hans on his side, as if they were in this together. Something about that made Hans uncomfortable. He didn't like feeling uncomfortable, so he decided not to investigate the feeling. It would pass. Almost everything did. "But I checked this whole place out, and I know how we can get out of here—but you have to get in there before someone comes along and sees you. Or trips over you or something."

That thought seemed to be enough to propel Regan forward, because he tried the door and slipped inside, easing it shut behind him. The Lieutenant's office was thankfully empty as the hallway outside, and surprisingly mundane, despite its reputation as a room prisoners walked into, but not out of. No medieval torture devices or bloodstains on the carpet. Sharpe did his favorite work elsewhere. This room was for inspection, determining if those unlucky enough to find themselves here would live long enough to see his truest and deadliest colors.

Ignoring the way his conscious brain wanted to break into panicked screaming at being in here at all, Hans floated over to the desk: paperless, clean, looked like it had never been used, because it hadn't, that wasn't this room's function. The only clues toward its real purpose were a pair of metal loops soldered into the desk's surface in two adjacent corners, conveniently spaced and sized for handcuffs.

Ignoring the troubling implications, Hans waved at the top drawer. "So, our way out is right in here. I'd do it myself, but you know, some stuff doesn't come that easy to ghosts."

Regan cautiously crept over and tried the drawer. It was locked, as Hans knew it was, and now Regan looked up at him with what looked like renewed panic as well as confusion.

"Now what?"

"Hold out your hand."

"What?" The frill of loose skin around Regan's neck gave a twitch, and it seemed like a nervous movement, because his yellow eyes grew wider and the vertical pupils thinner until they were little more than black slits.

"Trust me," Hans said, inwardly congratulating himself for his patience so far. "Just stick your hand right there over the drawer."

Cautiously, Regan did what he asked, and Hans did the same, placing his spectral hand over Regan's solid one. Regan shivered at the 'contact,' as if he'd just been caught in a cold wind, but didn't move— until Hans slammed both their hands down.

Regan let out a startled noise, almost a squeak, but his hand didn't smack against the desk. Instead, it passed through the surface with only the slightest resistance.

"What... in the..." He stared at where his wrist seemed to disappear into the solid metal.

"Pretty cool, huh?" Hans said with a grin. He never got tired of that. "I couldn't have done that on my own either. Thanks for the, uh, hand."

Slowly, Regan felt around inside the drawer, and picked up the only thing that seemed to be in it. Just as carefully, he pulled his hand back out with a slight shiver. In his hand was a small black cylinder with a red button on the top, like an explosive detonator out of a movie.

"Is this it?" Regan asked, holding it up gingerly, as if it might explode or burn him. "What is it?"

Hans grinned a little wider. "Push the button and find out."

"What'll happen if I do?"

Hans went through the motions of a sigh. His patience had limits, and too many questions was about the best way to reach them. Especially when he didn't have nearly as many answers. "If I'm right—which I am, I've been spying on these guys for like, ever—that's a mini site-to-site transporter. It should get us out of here."

"Where exactly is 'out of here?'" Regan pressed, clearly still suspicious. Great, that was just great. Hans had sprung him from the hot cell and guided him this far. What would it take to win his trust, or at least his cooperation?

"Just... out," Hans said, frustration flaring again. For some reason, he simply hadn't anticipated someone who would actually question his motives and not just accept the help without examining the why. Regan seemed smarter, or at least more anxious, than the average citizen. For Hans' purposes, that wasn't really a good thing. "Listen, I don't know, exactly, but it has to be better than getting caught here, right?"

"Yeah," Regan said, a visible shudder traveling through his entire body as if Hans' freezing touch had chilled him again. "Anything would."

He raised his thumb over the button, but then hesitated again. Hans was almost ready to prod him again so he didn't just stand there the whole night, waiting for the Lieutenant to come back to his office— but then Regan squeezed his eyes shut as if expecting a slap, and pressed the button.

The room dropped into darkness as quick as flicking a switch. When the light came back, it was blinding. Much brighter than anyone in Parole's eternally smoke-filled semi- twilight was used to, in the shadow of the barrier.

"We're... we're..." Regan said weakly, wavering on his feet and shielding his eyes.

"Yep," Hans said, doing his best to disguise his own disorientation and surprise—and most of all, his overwhelming relief. He'd been right. He'd gambled and won. Now he just needed to keep winning. "Take a good look."

They stood in a parking lot, surrounded by concrete barriers and military-looking vehicles, but on a raised platform like the roof of a parking garage. Looking dazed, Regan picked his way over to the edge where a concrete wall rose up chest-high, and peered over. Hans was already there, already staring.

Trees. Green leaves, not scorched and dead. Dry, dusty red rock giving way to near- desert, but for the first time in years the world stretched to the horizon. And overhead, a seemingly endless vault of the clear blue sky dotted with bunches of cumulous clouds. Nobody in

Parole had seen that particular color of blue in ten years. Hans had almost forgotten it existed too.

"This is... out," Regan said, shaky words carried on a cool breeze that made him shiver. He looked disoriented and dizzy, as if he'd climbed to the tallest point in Parole, and looked down. "This is *outside.*"

"Yep," Hans said, trying to project the illusion that he'd planned any of this, had any idea where the transport device would have taken them, and wasn't every bit as surprised to be outside as Regan was. That he wasn't making all of this up as he went. "Welcome to the real world."

The ground was damp despite the acrid surroundings and mostly-clear sky. It must have just rained. Regan slowly sucked in a deep breath, so hard Hans could hear the wheeze in his lungs.

In that moment, Hans was more envious of Regan than he had ever been of another human being—and he'd had years to be envious. People walking around in bodies, living their lives, taking their senses for granted, he would have given anything to be among them. But that was nothing compared to the jealousy he felt seeing the ecstasy on Regan's face, his utter wonder at the petrichor and smokeless air.

"It's nice, isn't it?" Hans said, abruptly jarring Regan back to the present after letting him enjoy the freedom for a few seconds. He looked startled, as if he'd forgotten Hans was there, and something about the shock on his face gave Hans a twisted little thrill of satisfaction. "So think about it. If I can get you out of the SkEye tower, where else can I get you?" He leaned in closer and gave Regan his best, winning, collaborative smile. "Fresh out of Parole."

Regan hesitated, looking up at him curiously. It wasn't the elation or desperation Hans expected to see on his face, and not for the first time he wondered if he'd made the right choice. "Why are you helping me?"

"You asked me that before," Hans evaded. He hadn't liked the question then either, and still didn't have the first idea of what would satisfy Regan's curiosity—or suspicion—and allow himself to retain the upper hand.

"And you never answered."

Damn. This guy was too quick for his own good, Hans thought with a stab of anxiety. Where was that nice Chrysedrine-induced delirium when he needed it?

"You think you're the only one who wants to get out of that death zone?" Hans said with a bitter chuckle that came too easily. But no matter how sarcastic he tended to sound by default now, his next words were the truth. "I didn't want to see anything really nasty happen to you back there. I've seen a lot of bad stuff go down here. But yeah, you got me, I'm not totally doing this out of the goodness of my heart. I'm, uh, hoping we can help each other."

"How?" Regan asked, starting to waver a little on his feet. He did seem dizzy, and Hans wondered how much functionality and lucidity he had left before the Chrysedrine withdrawal started to set in. But maybe it was just the shock of being outside. Hans was doing his best to play it cool, but if he'd had physical knees, they would've been weak too.

Hans gave him what he hoped was a confident, convincing, and enticingly enigmatic smile. "Push the button again."

After another moment of hesitation, Regan obeyed. The bright sky and cool air disappeared in an instant, replaced by parole's dull orange light and hot, suffocating smoke. Regan appeared a few inches above the ground and staggered on the sidewalk where he landed, obviously narrowly avoiding falling over.

"Back—we're back?" he gasped, as Hans readjusted to the new-old location as smoothly as possible. Once again his hunch had paid off. He tried to rid his mind of the fact that he'd really had no more idea where the transport device would have taken them this time than the last—or the fact that this was a random sidewalk instead of Sharpe's office—and instead focused on how well his luck was holding. "Where? How did—"

"Okay, remember that thing about not wanting anybody to come wandering over and trip over you?" Hans interrupted. Hopefully, he'd be able to keep Regan quiet and hidden before someone caught him. Hopefully, Regan wouldn't ask too many questions, or at least not pressure Hans for the answers. Hopefully, everything he'd worked for wouldn't be for nothing. "It gets a lot harder to avoid if you're yelling in the middle of the street. Hide, maybe?"

"Right, right, yeah," Regan said, turning partly invisible again—his body must have still been too ravaged by Chrysedrine and Sharpe to maintain a full fade—and slipping into the nearest narrow space between two crumbling buildings. Once hidden, he let out a choked, wild laugh. "I can't believe it. I still can't believe we were just *outside!*"

"Yeah," said Hans, not needing to force the self-satisfaction in his voice. So far, so good. "It was pretty amazing, right?"

"Amazing doesn't even begin," Regan said, holding up the small transport device and looking at it like it was made of solid gold and diamonds. Or maybe water—much more valuable in Parole. "And it's all thanks to this. This, right here, this is our way out!"

"Well, about that..."

Hans clamped an icy hand over Regan's again. This time, he didn't plunge the green, physical hand through another corporeal surface. Instead, he made Regan's fingers tighten their grip on the transport device—so strong and sudden that the black plastic crumbled in his hand

"Hey!" Regan yelped, jumping as his hand crushed the object. Looking almost comically shocked, he stared at Hans, then at the remains of the device, then back at him. "Why'd you do that? That could've—"

"Fallen into the wrong hands, and been a disaster," Hans said quickly, hoping Regan was still drugged enough not to question his shaky logic. There were more transport devices where that thing had come from—but if Regan started to think for a second that he didn't need Hans to get to them, there went almost all his leverage. He'd get more, Hans would keep looking for advantages, but this one had practically fallen into his lap, and he wasn't letting it go that easily. "All that matters now is that SkEye is down one mini teleporter thingy—and now you know I'm the real deal."

"I have to get home," Regan said faintly, rubbing his wrist where Hans had touched him again.

The way he'd reacted before, it seemed like Hans' touch was freezing, or shocking, or something unpleasant at any rate. Something about that made Hans feel dully... what? Disappointed? Regretful? He couldn't imagine anyone actually enjoying his touch, and that made him feel...

Hans didn't recognize the emotion, but he knew he didn't enjoy it, so he pushed it away.

"I have to find my—friends," Regan continued, casting a wary look up at Hans. He was definitely afraid of him, or at least not at all comfortable. That was fine, he didn't have to be. Better if he had a healthy fear of Hans, anyway, he'd be a lot more likely to cooperate. "They'll be looking for me."

"What, nervous about them meeting me?" Hans laughed, though that same unidentified but unpleasant feeling lingered in the back of his mind. Couldn't be that he still wanted human connection, after all this time. That wouldn't help him achieve his goals at all. So he wouldn't pay it any attention. "I wouldn't worry about that. I'm probably not even real. This is all in your head, right?"

Hans laughed, and it came a little easier. He had the situation well in hand. Even if he didn't exactly know what to do next, he'd figure it out. He always did.

"But yeah, you'd better get moving. Who knows when SkEye will figure out you're gone?"

Regan didn't answer, and it looked to Hans like he was gathering all his strength to make his next move. When he stepped forward, it was on unsteady feet, looking like he'd be lucky to make it half a block before he collapsed entirely.

Not my problem, Hans resolved. He'd done his part, laid the groundwork. The rest was up to Regan. Assuming he lived—which, if he actually had people out looking for him, was a lot more likely than it might have been—Hans would have everything he needed to not only escape Parole, but everything else that haunted his dreams like he haunted Regan right now.

This would be fine, Hans thought. This was all according to plan.

"I always knew it would come to this," Ash said as he and Celeste made their way through Parole's smoky streets, covering the same ground for what had to be the fourth time over the past two days. "We all come into this knowing the risks. Doesn't make it any easier, but at least we've had a while to prepare. If you ever can."

In the pre-sunrise gray, the area was thankfully deserted, but no people meant no clues toward the one person they wanted to find. Ash's four-fingered hand kept absently reaching up to tug on the shark's tooth that hung around his neck on a chain, an unconscious nervous habit. It didn't usually bother him, but right now, considering what they may be up against, he wouldn't mind shaking this particular tic.

"He's not dead yet," Celeste said, level and straightforward as ever, and just as hard to read. Her helmet's shining black visor revealed nothing of her face; the only hint of any kind of personal style was the silver star decals on her earpieces. Even her voice was clearly modulated and disguised, the distortion leaving it unsettlingly free of expression.

"They've had him for two days. No use in pretending that's not a possibility," Ash said, uncharacteristically dour himself. He cast her a sideways glance. "But that's not quite what I mean. You know what I... do, right?"

"I've heard about it," she replied, not looking up at him or slowing her purposeful strides. "You serve a morbid but very necessary function."

"Hey, it's not always morbid," he said a little defensively. "Not everyone I extract is dead, they just would've been in about a minute if I hadn't gotten there."

"You don't need to explain yourself to me. Parole's an unforgiving sandbox to play in. People get into tight spots, they need a helping hand. Or, failing that..."

"Right," Ash said, a little downcast. He'd been keeping a pretty good pace so far, but scouring the city on too little sleep and too much adrenaline was starting to wear on him. "Failing that, they need to disappear. Even death won't stop SkEye from chasing us, so, evidence cleaned up, bodies given up to the fire. It's better than the alternative. Letting SkEye use us against each other..."

"Yes," Celeste said, and now he almost caught a hint of *something* under the vocal distortion, a wavering it couldn't quite disguise. "They did it once with Mihir. Never again."

"No," he said, quietly resolved. "And definitely not this time. But my point is, I've done this for years. It means accepting the reality that

I'll probably have to extract people I love, whether they're alive or not. And if they're not, I know what I have to..." he was quiet for a few seconds and she didn't push him. "It just doesn't make it any easier. You'd think it would, after all this time, but no."

"If it ever got easier, that's when I'd worry," she said, and it was about the closest to comforting her strangely modulated voice ever got. "But we all know the realities and risks. Regan knows them. If he could speak to us, I know he'd want you to—"

She stopped walking, head tilted slightly, apparently listening to something Ash couldn't hear. He stopped too but didn't question, just waiting.

"Ah," Celeste said after a few seconds. "There's been an escape. Detention center about a mile back."

In a heartbeat, Ash's despair turned to electrifying hope. "That's our boy!" he exclaimed, turning 180 degrees and starting off running with renewed vigor. "Let's find him before someone else does."

Regan continued through the smoke-charred streets in nothing but his dirty and scorched paper clothes, feeling like every step might be his last. The pavement burned hot against his bare feet and the acrid air stung with every inhale. He would have given a lot for a glass of water, or a breathing mask. Either of them were worth many times their weight in gold in Parole, and he had neither.

But he did have a constant guide and companion, who talked to him—or at him, given Regan's inability to form more than a few words at a time—every step of the way.

"Better, right?" Hans chattered as they moved, floating easily alongside him. "Sure feels good to be out of that prison cell. And didn't that fresh air smell lovely? Didn't the sun feel good on your skin? Not like I'd know how any of that feels," he finished bitterly.

"Where do I go from here?" Regan asked wearily, reaching the end of one alley and looking up both ways down the thankfully quiet street.

"Huh? Oh, hell if I know," Hans answered, a little too quickly. "I got you out of that detention facility, my work here's done."

Regan stopped, looking up at his strange rescuer who he was starting to doubt more with every step. "Then why are you still following me?"

"Because I do have some other, uh, unfinished business," Hans snickered. "Ghost humor. Anyway, I just did you a few very generous solids, my dude. Without me, you'd still be shackled and trapped, probably with a few more needles in you."

"What's your point?" Regan asked, suspicion growing along with an unpleasant wave of anxiety. It felt hot and sick and made his already-spinning head feel a little lighter.

"I granted your wish," Hans said, and now there was no trace of his usually ever-present smirk. "So now I'd say you owe me."

"What do you want?" Definitely nauseous. Definitely dizzy. Definitely back on the defensive, because of course Hans wanted something. People always wanted something, usually things Regan had no intention or ability to give.

"Mm, well, let me answer that question with one of mine," Hans said with a tilt of his partially-transparent head. "You'd do anything to escape this place, right?"

"Anything's... a lot of things," Regan said with a harsh cough. The world was starting to tilt as well as spin, and the smoggy air burned all the way down his throat. "And there's lots of things... that I wouldn't..."

"Are you kidding?" Hans laughed. "Look at yourself. All burned and drugged, no clothes, no help, no hope. Don't you want to fight back against the people who did this to you?"

"I do have help. And hope." The world spun a little faster. Regan didn't know if the ground was moving underneath him, or he was the one weaving erratically. His head burned with fever, and his stomach was starting to cramp, enough to make him stop walking and try to massage the painful tension. He coughed again and it hurt his throat.

"Well, doesn't look that way from where I'm floating," Hans observed, clearly noticing Regan's increasing dizziness. "I'd say you still need my help. And, if I'm being honest here, I could really use yours."

"Wh—what..." Regan couldn't get the full sentence out before another coughing fit overwhelmed him, throat frighteningly tight.

"Oh, don't worry about that for now," Hans said lightly. "Just keep everything I've said in mind. You can just owe me a favor. Later, once you're not about to keel over."

"I'm not..." Regan tried, but couldn't push the words out past the awful hacking cough. He wasn't promising anything. He didn't like the sound of any of this. He didn't trust Hans for a second. Even if the strange ghost boy had guided him out of the detention center, it seemed like all of that was just to serve his own mysterious agenda. And Regan had had enough of people using him to last a lifetime.

And then there was the thought that made him shiver despite Parole's heat and his own fever.

Regan didn't even know if Hans was real.

Was *any* of this real? Was he still back in that cell, alone with Sharpe, a needle in his thigh, Chrysedrine raging through his veins and making every cell burst into frantic, brilliant, deadly ecstasy?

"Okay, that's about my cue," Hans said, starting to float up and away, becoming a little less solid every second. "I'll see you later. Remember what I said—you owe me."

Before Regan could protest, or catch his breath, Hans was gone. Within seconds it was like he'd never been there at all, like he was nothing more than a hallucination or bad dream that followed Regan even after he woke up. But even if Hans wasn't real, some of this was. That glimpse of the world beyond the barrier had been so real. So vital. Regan couldn't ignore the precious second of *outside*, the sun, the fresh, clean, beautiful *air...*

No air.

Regan thought he heard another voice, not Hans, someone familiar—but he could make no sense of it, finally overcome by Chrysedrine's sudden onslaught and just-as-sudden withdrawal. He was already falling.

"We've been here already," Celeste pointed out as they passed the hollowed-out shell of what had once been an apartment complex.

"We've been a lot of places already," Ash said absently, still fiddling with his necklace chain. He'd been doing that almost nonstop since they'd begun the search. That and imagining every worst possible consequence of every minute Regan stayed missing. "Two days is a long time to look for someone. But it's a longer time for SkEye to have him in a hot cell."

"This would be much easier if we had any way to track him."

"You've said, and I agree," Ash acknowledged, hoping his oxygen mask also masked some of his fatigue and worry-fueled annoyance. "But if he hadn't crushed his monitor, they'd be able to track him too, assuming he still had it. Or they could have backwards traced it, followed it right to CyborJ, and that's the opposite of what anyone needs right now. Regan knew that. He did the right thing. If that makes our job harder..."

"I suppose the fact that we can't find him is a good sign," Celeste said, though she sounded as impassive as usual. "I've heard nothing more on scanners, so they don't have him yet either. I can't think of many people harder to find than a man who can quite literally disappear whenever he wants. Chances are, he's still alive, but those chances weaken with every—"

"Look!" Ash stopped, flinging one arm out in front of her as if they were in a car and he'd just slammed the brakes. "There, up ahead!"

On the ashy ground a few yards away, something phased in and out of visibility, green skin and once-white paper gown, now scorched and covered with dirt. Ash felt a rare-for- Parole chill as he pounded up to the unmistakable form, Celeste silently running beside him. He'd seen Regan turn invisible many times, but always all at once, never halfway or sporadically like this, image flickering like a badly tuned ancient antenna TV.

"Regan? Can you hear—I think he's unconscious, but he's breathing," Ash said, removing his own oxygen mask to place it over Regan's face. He'd be fine without it until they got home but Regan might not be. He gingerly slid his arms under Regan's shoulders and knees. Regan's asthma was usually controlled enough for him to not only safely exist in Parole, but run around at night scaling buildings. But that was with good oxygen, with medication, and not after days of imprisonment and possible torture. Probable torture. "Oh, God, buddy, what did they do to you?"

"Do you want my actual guess?" Celeste asked, black visor inscrutable as ever as she surveyed Regan, who started to squirm as if pained where he was touched.

"Sorry, sorry," Ash said quietly, lifting Regan as gently as possible and holding him against his chest, just beneath where the huge shark-like tooth necklace hung. Then he turned to Celeste, looking almost afraid of what she might say. "No thank you. I have a pretty good idea too. I just hope it's not as bad as it looks."

"Radio Angel?" Celeste said, tilting her head to reopen the channel, and falling into step beside Ash as he strode quickly back into the alley shadows Regan appeared to have just emerged from before collapsing. "Good news. We've found him. He's alive. Tell everyone we're on our way home."

Kari's joyful voice vaguely registered as Ash kept his eyes on Regan, but he didn't hear the words, freeing one hand to gently slide the other under his neck frill, feeling a rapid, thready pulse. His scaly skin burned hot, unnaturally so even for Parole. Ash had never actually seen Regan sweat, and wasn't entirely sure if he even could, because with a fever like the one he was running, anyone else would have been drenched. There wasn't much need for jackets in scorched Parole, but Ash wished for one to wrap Regan up in now, anything better than the torn and burned paper gown. He trembled in Ash's arms, shivering like he was caught in an icy winter wind.

"It's gonna be okay now," Ash promised quietly. "We're gonna get you home and take good care of you. You'll be fine, and everyone's gonna be so glad to see you. Jay's gonna be there—he's fine, by the way, don't worry about that. You did the right thing. You kept him safe."

Hearing Ash speak and feeling the vibrations in his chest seemed to be doing Regan some good, because he stopped squirming and his shakes began to gradually subside. He might be unconscious, but Ash kept talking, even if Regan couldn't understand the words. They both needed to hear them.

"Zilch came out to look for you too, but they'll meet us back home. Rowan too, and they're gonna fix you up, nice and easy. They're gonna be so happy to see you too, and proud of you. Two whole days in lockup, surviving God knows what." His own throat was getting a little scratchy from the smoky air—how Regan had lasted this long out here, with his less-than-healthy lungs, was beyond him—but he kept talking. "And Annie! She'll be..." he stopped, shoulders sagging a little. "Maybe we wait until you're doing a little better for Annie to see you. I know you'll understand that. But when she can, she'll be—"

"No!" Regan whimpered, taking him by surprise. He pushed weakly at Ash's chest as if trying to get away or sit up, recoiling from—

"Oh, God, I'm sorry," Ash said, stricken, and quickly freed his hand again to tuck the huge, sharpened tooth back inside his shirt, hiding it from view. Regan was shaking again, hiding his face against Ash's arm and clutching him, fingernails digging in a little. "I'm so sorry, buddy. I should've known better."

"We did know better," Celeste said. "Or at least suspected, after that 'blood in the water' business. I'd say now we know for sure. Sharpe was... involved."

"We definitely do not know that for sure," Ash shot back, frustrated at the desperation in his own voice, but trying to keep it low to avoid scaring Regan even further. He'd started out objective and realistic, but finding Regan alive had gone a long way toward resurrecting his hard-dying optimism. But facing the possibility of Regan being dead, and Regan being captured by Sharpe were two different things. Somehow, the second one was worse. "Sharpe always leaves his victims in... a lot worse of shape."

"He may be injured in ways we can't see," Celeste maintained, still sounding unconvinced and grim.

"Well, he's not bleeding out all over the street." Ash couldn't tell the extent of Regan's injuries, not here, and not under all the dirt and Parole soot. But he knew the scenes of Sharpe's crimes tended to be bloody, unforgettable, and unmistakable. "Listen, if Sharpe had him, we'd know. Besides, Regan's never liked that tooth, and he's a little out of it right now. I'm not jumping to the worst possible conclusion, not yet. Not until he tells us otherwise."

Celeste didn't reply, but Ash was sure he caught the slightest shake in the hands she curled into loose fists, an uneasy shift to her spine even as she stood a little more ramrod- straight.

"He'll be fine," Ash said, voice softening, every bit as much to convince himself as Celeste. She needed it as much as he did, he knew, and was equally unlikely to admit it. "Whether Sharpe had him or not, he's alive. It didn't happen again. We didn't lose anyone else."

Celeste cast him a sidelong glance, and Ash caught a flash of Regan's battered reflection in her visor. "Not yet."

Ash let out a long sigh that carried two solid days' worth of tension and furious helplessness. He resisted the urge to hold Regan closer to his chest and risk hurting him further. "Not yet. But we got him back. Now he has a chance."

"You do sound a bit more optimistic than before," she observed, and he noted that the same was true for her even under its electronic alterations.

"Yeah, well," he said, looking down at Regan's face. "Bringing someone home alive... it's more than I can say for my job most nights. I'm counting this as a win."

"Well, all right," Celeste said, and now Ash could hear the smile in her voice even if he couldn't see it. For a moment, she wasn't just the hardened, masked agent they knew but didn't really know. He thought of Annie's crooked grins that made her look so much younger, and, not for the first time, wondered how old Celeste actually was under that helmet, and the years of horrors that left none of them untouched or unchanged. "I suppose we've earned that much."

Regan had stopped his fitful squirming and turned toward Ash's chest, burying his face in his shirt. The tooth remained just behind the fabric, but Regan remained still, and seemed at least a little more tranquil. It was almost like he knew who was holding him and where they were going. Another tiny win. Once they got home, everything would change again, and they'd face a whole new set of challenges and fears and possible devastation. But for now, in the time between finding him alive and whatever came next, Ash held Regan safe and tried to appreciate every step.

Withdrawal

JUST UNDER A MONTH BEFORE CHAMELEON MOON

Zilch didn't stop running until they reached the library and burst inside. They didn't usually move fast—fortunately, as it was a terrifying sight—but today was the exception that took them halfway across Parole faster than some could have made the trip in cars, since Zilch didn't need to slow down for things like perilous trenches or piles of debris. Now, the juggernaut in black rags barreled through the library stacks, paced impatiently on the freight elevator ride down, and shot out into the dark underground hallway the moment the doors opened. They tore down the corridor and around corners, only coming to a halt when they

reached a door, and someone sitting hunched over in a folding chair just outside it.

"In there?" they asked as Ash sat up straight and raised his head from where it had been resting on his forearms.

"Yeah," he said, weariness tangible in his voice, the hunch of his back, and the dark circles under his usually-bright blue eyes. "Rowan's got him. Jay was helping them get ready, but I don't think he was up to actually seeing—anyway, I'd just be in the way too, too many people in one—"

Zilch didn't even wait for him to finish the sentence. By the time Ash stopped talking and put his head back down, they were already inside.

They finally came to a stop at the side of a bed in the small room that functioned as the library's secondary medical site. Most non-urgent treatment happened downstairs in the common area that served as sleeping and temporary living quarters for Parole's traumatized and displaced citizens, but this room was reserved for privacy, and more serious cases that shouldn't be exposed to the general public.

This was one of those cases.

"How is he?" Zilch asked, staring down at Regan's unconscious face, taking in the ragged, shallow rise and fall of his chest, the tremors that ran down his arms and made his fingers twitch, and the unhealthy gray cast of his green, scaly skin even under the coating of oily soot. He must have collapsed somewhere outside. Regan didn't really sweat—something that had become quickly apparent in forever-hot Parole soon after his transformation—but if he could, he'd almost certainly be sweating as well as shaking.

"His heart's racing, and he hasn't regained consciousness," Rowan said, looking up from where they'd been taking Regan's pulse, two fingers on the inside of his wrist.

It probably would have been easier to feel for the pulse point on his neck under his frill, but the loose skin was shaking too much, like a leaf in a breeze. Regan might not sweat, but Rowan certainly did—still, that was their only outward sign of anxiety, their voice clear and calm and movements smooth.

"It could just be shock and dehydration, that's what I'm hoping," Rowan continued, and somehow they made it sound so reasonable, as if Regan wasn't lying here halfway between dead and alive. "He definitely had an asthma attack, he needs oxygen and albuterol at least, but I need to know more of what we're dealing with first. Now that you're here, I'll feel better taking care of that, and getting this—this *thing* off of him."

They picked at the flimsy paper gown Regan wore, as if it were something distasteful like a large stinging insect. The thin material was filthy and torn, and scorched as if it had caught fire at several points. There were a couple possible explanations for that, and Zilch didn't like any of them.

"Waiting was the right choice," Zilch said, forcing themself to say the words and stay present, not to get lost in trying to figure out what had happened to Regan, and what may still. "He might wake up."

"Disoriented and hurting in a room he might not remember, with no clothes," Rowan confirmed with a nod, on Zilch's same page as ever. "I'm glad you're here."

"What can I do?" Zilch asked as Rowan stepped away toward an array of medical tools that Zilch did their best not to look at. It wasn't that they were squeamish; they were no stranger to frightening implements and the experience of having their own parts removed and replaced while fully conscious. They were long since caring about the idiosyncrasies of their own body. Regan was a much different story. He'd feel everything.

"Just... hold his hands," Rowan said, coming back with a large pair of scissors, one of the less-ominous things they could have picked up at least. Rowan's hands were steady as they always were, but Zilch still couldn't help the pang of anxiety as the scissors opened and slipped under the gown's neck. "I don't want him waking up or jerking in the middle of this and getting hurt."

Zilch gently took both of Regan's trembling hands in theirs, and even their own reanimated hands could feel the unnatural heat coming off him. Running a fever, a bad one, if Zilch noticed it. Rowan started to snip through the paper rags at Regan's shoulder and gently peel them off, revealing more unhealthily grey-green skin. Zilch looked every bit of it over carefully, searching for bruises, cuts, burns, or anything else to indicate what had happened to Regan, but aside from the grayish tone, they saw nothing unusual. No immediately obvious injuries—a good thing on the surface, but Zilch didn't trust it. Some of the worst injuries weren't immediately visible, and not just in an emotional sense.

Rowan continued, finding no clues until they exposed Regan's right upper thigh. There, his skin was almost its normal color, but even brighter than usual, more vibrant, somehow healthier. Zilch leaned a bit closer, puzzled, looking for any sign of injury in or around the green spot, but finding nothing else suspicious.

"Oh," Rowan said, more of a gasp than a word, and Zilch looked sharply up. They didn't look confused as much as alarmed, one hand covering their mouth, the other one still holding the scissors but not cutting anymore. Their face had gone pale, skin suddenly drained of color almost as much as Regan's.

"What is it?" Zilch asked warily. The sense of dread they felt now was so powerful that they knew the question was ultimately unnecessary. Even safe in its jar some floors away, their brain was trying to protect them from the horrible answer. That didn't stop them from needing to hear it confirmed beyond all doubt or hope. "What does it mean?"

"No injuries—or healed injuries, so neatly they're undetectable," Rowan said, voice tense, and obviously forcing themself to put the scissors down and remove the remainders of Regan's ruined paper gown. "Shaking, sweating, fever, trouble breathing. With one part of the body actually enhanced, strengthened. Or rather, his *ability* strengthened. The ability granted by..."

"Chrysedrine," Zilch said, tightening their hold on both of Regan's hands as if he might vanish.

"Yes," Rowan said, sounding breathless, but still moving in a deliberate, controlled way as they dropped the remains of the burned gown into a waste bin and set down the scissors. "I was afraid of this. But it didn't seem likely, SkEye's goal was always to interrogate and—and eliminate him, since they knew they'd never get him back under control, and Sharpe—if it really was Sharpe—he was never that... subtle. I thought if he had Regan, we'd know immediately."

"He did," Zilch said in a rasping whisper that did nothing to communicate the wave of panic and fury sweeping through them. "Regan's worst nightmare. Sharpe got his hands on him. Sharpe had him in a room. Whatever he did, the Chrysedrine removed the evidence."

"But now we know what we're dealing with, and knowledge is power," Rowan said, determined calm taking over again. They went over to their gathered equipment and came back with an oxygen tank and attached plastic mask. "Chrysedrine addiction—and withdrawal. Can you help me...?"

Together they eased Regan under the covers, pulling the clean white sheets up to his chest but leaving half of it and his arms free. Anything else might have kept him too hot, kept his fever up, Zilch thought, because that was easier to think about than the reason Regan's skin burned even at their somewhat numbed touch.

"So we know he probably doesn't have any further physical injuries," Rowan said, clearly trying to get their own thoughts in order and prevent themself from descending into panic. They were doing a better job than Zilch, whose dulled affect just hid it better. "The Chrysedrine will have healed them, even internal bleeding. So we focus on the withdrawal in the long term, and in the short term, helping however we immediately can. Like helping him breathe."

They picked up the plastic mask and started to gently fit it over Regan's face—then stopped when Regan began to squirm, head turning away and frill jerking in an agitated spasm. He still didn't seem conscious, pulled listlessly against Zilch's hands. It was like he was trying to rip his own hands free, but couldn't find the strength. Zilch didn't even need to hold him down; Regan was clearly unable to do anything beyond weak struggles, but just as obviously agitated and protesting the mask.

"Ahh, sorry, sorry," Rowan said, removing it immediately. "I forgot. Sorry."

Zilch gave Rowan a confused look. They both knew Regan's idiosyncrasies and preferences, particularly important ones like this—he could tolerate putting on an oxygen mask for outdoor runtimes, but he had to be the one to put it on, in control and free to remove it. Someone else covering his face could send him into a panic attack, especially while this vulnerable. Rowan should have known that. Any other time they would have.

But now they detached the full-face mask and, within seconds, had replaced it with a simple pronged nozzle that fit inside the nostrils, and tried again. This didn't seem to disturb Regan nearly as much, though he still shook and squirmed fitfully for a few seconds. Eventually, he fell back into stillness and deep unconsciousness, this time with less labored breathing.

"There is enough air," Zilch whispered, still stroking the back of Regan's hand with their thumb.

The familiar words always brought Regan comfort, but they didn't do much for Zilch right now. If Rowan heard, they didn't give any indication, and for a while, the small room was silent.

"How do we get him through this?" Zilch asked after a few painful seconds, keeping their voice low. Even in his struggles, Regan had shown no sign of waking up so far, but they still didn't want to risk disturbing him before he was ready.

"In any other case—with anyone else—I'd get them another Chrysedrine dose, and taper them off slowly. Over two weeks at least, and even that's pushing it. With Regan, that's not an option." Rowan gave Zilch a sideways, half-hopeful look. "Unless he's said anything different to you."

Zilch shook their head. "No. 'Never again.' He's said that for eight years."

"The same to me. So all we can really do is control the symptoms, and let it run its course. Keep his fever down, give him oxygen, try to keep his heart and blood pressure from skyrocketing out of control. If we keep him within reasonable limits, help him regain some homeostasis, his own system will take over." Rowan cast a brief look at Regan's face, but turned away just as quickly, their own face a careful neutral. "After that, it's up to him."

"There's nothing we can give him that would help?"

"We could keep him sedated through the worst of it," Rowan said, not sounding overly excited at the idea. "But I don't think we should do that until Jay's seen him at least—but he's on his way."

"Why wait?" Zilch asked, watching Regan's breathing even out. The purified oxygen was doing him some good at least. "Shouldn't he sleep through as much as he can?"

"If we put him under any further than he already is..." Rowan stopped. When they didn't continue after a few seconds, Zilch looked up to see worry clear on their face, the first real break in their practiced professional calm so far. "I'm not sure he'll wake up."

"What are his chances?" Zilch asked, terrified to hear the actual answer, but needing to even more.

"I'm going to assume they gave him pure Chrysedrine, not a street knockoff, which would probably have killed him by now." Rowan hesitated and the controlled anxiety on their face intensified. "The withdrawal survival rate is around seventy-five percent."

"Better than it could be," Zilch said with a nod, relieved, but still watching Rowan with some confusion. They didn't seem nearly as convinced. "He survived this once, he can do it again."

Rowan didn't answer immediately, staring not at Regan, but at a spot on the opposite wall. They didn't look nervous anymore, instead seeming calm once again, but in a detached, distant kind of way.

"Surviving it once—it doesn't mean it'll happen again. The body is even more hyper-reactive to Chrysedrine after the first exposure. Everyone I saw survive—they made it through their *first* withdrawal. This will be Regan's second, and the odds of surviving a second withdrawal after a re-addiction… do not go up."

"How many people have you seen make it through the second?" Zilch asked, sensing that this was the real heart of the matter, on which everything else hinged. Rowan hesitated again, and Zilch looked up at them, their next question more urgent. "How many, Rowan?"

Rowan briefly shut their eyes, just long enough to take in a deep breath and let it out. "None."

None. Zilch had suspected that answer earlier, but rejected it. And they rejected it now.

"He'll make it." Zilch said firmly, refusing to acknowledge any other possibility even to themself. They reached out and put one large, grey hand on Rowan's back and started to rub it in a slow circle. "You've got him. There's no safer place he could be."

Rowan didn't pull away, but they did look up, and the clear distress on their face made Zilch stop, and hold still. "Zilch, I love you so much, and I appreciate what you're trying to do, but, until he's safe, don't— don't talk to me about anything… emotional. I need to stay focused and clear to give Regan his best possible chance, and I can't do that and *feel* at the same time. And I'm feeling a lot already."

"Understood," Zilch said, and withdrew their hand, strangely conflicted when Rowan visibly relaxed. That was the complete opposite of what usually happened. Every other time, their tension melted away as soon as Zilch touched them. That more than anything confirmed the seriousness of this situation, the strangeness, and the fragility. It made Zilch's heart sink, figuratively speaking. Maybe once it was over they could get back to normalcy, but nothing about this was normal, especially not Regan lying here shaking.

Zilch sloped back over to stand by Regan again, taking his hand in theirs and running their thumb over the too-hot skin of his knuckles.

They didn't say it out loud, since this particular thought was emotionally-charged indeed, Zilch did affirm it to themself, willing Regan to somehow hear and understand.

We did it once. You can still do it again.

"Let me in!" Annie shouted, trying for the fourth time to slip past Ash and through the door standing between her and Regan. So far she'd been unsuccessful. For someone so unfairly tall and muscled, and wearing such big clompy boots, Ash was surprisingly agile, and dedicated to his cause. "Why are you keeping me out here?"

"Because we'd just be in the way," Ash said, putting both large hands on her narrow shoulders gently enough to not cause any pain to her unsteady joints, but firmly enough to keep her in place. "And I mean both of us. I'm not in there for a reason too."

"You mean besides keeping me out?" Her voice caught, and she was going to cry, wasn't she? She'd be so mad if she cried, madder than she was at Ash, but not as furious as she was at whoever had done this to Regan in the first place.

"Yeah," Ash said with a too-reasonable nod. Perhaps unconsciously, he tucked the large shark tooth he wore on a chain around his neck into his shirt, but quickly replaced his hand on her shoulder. "I have no idea what to do in this situation, and there's about a million ways that me trying to help would just make everything worse. Rowan knows how to handle this, and they're gonna do their best."

"What about Zilch?" Annie protested. "They're not a doctor!"

"*You* try getting Zilch away from Regan," Ash laughed, but it wasn't an entirely happy sound. "They're a lot harder to move than you. Besides... Regan just tends to do better with them around, even if he's not conscious. I figure it's like what they say about people being in a coma, even if they're out, they can still kind of hear and sense what's going on around them."

"And me being in there wouldn't help?" Annie had stopped fighting him, and now folded her arms across her chest, hunching a little like she wanted to curl up into a ball right there.

"It's not that, Spark Plug," Ash said more gently. "I just want to let them work without distractions... and when we do see Regan, I want us to see him better and doing okay. Chrysedrine withdrawal is ugly. He'll be fine, but it's not going to be fun getting there, that's all."

"Regan's family," Annie said, giving a loud sniff and blinking hard. She kept fighting tears, but it was an increasingly losing battle. "If he's dying, don't keep me away from him. Don't tell me I can't say goodbye."

He gave her shoulders a little squeeze, which helped ground her a little. The reassuring feeling of nine fingers was a comfort that specifically meant him. "We're not there yet, and if we were, Rowan would be the one calling us in. But we're not gonna be. We got him home and that was the hardest part, but there's nothing either of us can do here except for be here for him when he wakes up. Try to have a little faith, yeah?"

Annie didn't answer but she nodded, head hanging low. She pushed one last time but now it wasn't to reach the door. She stepped forward until her body hit his and buried her face in his chest; his arms immediately went around her.

"I know it's tough. But we've gotten out of worse. Remember that."

Regan remembers.

He remembers the first time he heard that voice, nowhere near as soft and warm as it is now, even heard faintly through a door. Ash can be a force when he's angry, or when he's protecting his family and home, and that's how Regan met him. His first impression of Ash eight years ago is a blurred image as he tries to keep his eyes open, panting and shivering in Zilch's arms as they stand in the library doorway and ask him to please, please let them inside.

His first withdrawal. The most intense agony he's felt in his life until that point. And never since, not until right now.

He'd thought he was ready to leave SkEye. To take the opportunity Zilch had given them, at their own peril, and Garrett had facilitated. To run, save who they could—three children, it should have been four, but something went wrong— and not look back. Maybe he was ready at the time, but he wasn't for what came after. Nobody could be ready for Chrysedrine withdrawal.

He hadn't been ready for how quickly it came on. It had only been two, three days since his last dose, but he'd gone long enough to feel the beginning pangs before. But the intensity had gone from zero to unbearable in the space of a few hours, and soon he understood how SkEye had them all so firmly under their thumb, how completely their lives were owned and controlled. He hadn't been ready to fully collapse, legs giving out under him, only avoiding a painful fall to the ground because Zilch was there to catch him, like they always were.

Then he's half-blind and too dizzy to know which way is up by the time they reach the large, reinforced stronghold, the library. He realizes he's lying in a bed, shaking so hard his bones feel like they're going to separate, wracked by tremors and so hot at the same time. His face and arms are numb but his marrow is on fire and soon his skin will crack and peel, scorched from the inside.

It's a strange room but he's not alone in it; he can hear Zilch's voice not far off, but he can't see them. They're arguing with someone—or someone's arguing with them, tone harsh, words clipped, a wall standing between them and safety that melds with a much happier version of Ash's voice in his mind. It's strange to remember they're one and the same.

But they're not getting kicked out either. He doesn't know what Zilch says to get the people in the library to let them stay—or maybe it's Garrett's verbal gymnastics and transactional brilliance that saves them once again—but hours go by and he's still in this bed, slipping into unconsciousness and awoken by his own violent shakes and gasps.

He's not alone. There's a little girl watching, she thinks he doesn't see her, and he wonders if she's even real. Later he finds out her name, and thinks that no one in their right mind would mistake Annie for anything but the completely forthright, honest and unafraid child she is, too old-souled and down-to-earth to be *a specter—but he wasn't in his right mind at the time.*

Then someone's taking her hand, saying the first words he understands in hours—"Annie, no, you don't want to see this. Let's find your mom"—and his eyes slip shut again. When they open again—a second later? An hour?—there's someone standing over him and again he's not sure how much is real and how much is his tortured brain filling in blanks where it has no business improvising.

He's seen unique, beautiful and frightening Chrysedrine mutations, some even as extreme as his own, but never someone with large, curling black ram's horns, or heard hooves instead of footsteps when they move. Never met someone like this at all. They're exactly the kind of person SkEye doesn't want to exist except to serve as their tools. They're like him.

"Hi there. Looks like you're starting to come out of it." They're looking at him in a way that's different from the distrustful man at the door, or the little girl's undisguised, wary fascination. Curious but not judging, and the closest thing to gentle he's seen since Zilch set him down.

Regan tries to speak and the sound that comes out of his mouth scares him; it's a rough cough that sneaks up on him and hurts his throat. He feels a shiver rush over him and doesn't know if it's his invisibility startle reflex, or just another wave of withdrawal tremors.

"It's okay, you don't have to talk," says the person with the horns, and he doesn't remember them moving, but they're holding a glass of water now. Clear and shining and worth more than anyone who'd never lived in Parole would believe. Wonder of wonders, it even has a straw. Regan's throat is so dry and painful he almost cries at the sight, but he's probably too dehydrated to shed a tear. "But you should drink. It's okay, just relax..."

It's lukewarm and has a vaguely antiseptic taste—most water that isn't handed out from SkEye's rations does, the hallmark of homemade purification systems even rarer than the water itself—but it's the most beautiful thing Regan has ever tasted. It tastes like life and the knowledge that he's still in it, and the hope that he might have more life in him yet.

The horned person helps him sit up and drink more, and maybe it's the way his head starts spinning again the moment he's anywhere close to upright, but they're beautiful too. If this is a hallucination, it's not a bad one, but he hopes for the first time that it's not.

Just one thing poisons the rare, not-painful moment in this Hell.

Something's not right, besides the obvious, he's sure, he doesn't know why, but he knows it.

Something's gone wrong, and it's all to do with that first moment, him in the bed and Rowan with the water in one hand and his heart in the other.

Suddenly he's terrified that it never happened, or not the way he remembers, something's changed, and he doesn't know how that could be when everything about that day rings as true as ever, but he can't stop worrying. It's like a step in his mind that he misses, sending him falling into a place that's dark and cold and—

Rowan isn't there.

Something tells him they're gone. Or they never were here. It's a horrible, all-encompassing void that feels like a black hole, the absence of warmth and light and an overwhelming gravitational pull, drawing everything into its all-devouring maw and crushing it into nothing.

But he doesn't have time to dwell on the strange and unpleasant feeling, *because he's somewhere else now, with someone else, a voice clear and constant in his ear, the way it's always been.*

&

Jay's voice is always so immediate, so unmistakable, and not just because it's one of the most distinctive and expressive and attractive things about him, something Regan would recognize anywhere, in any world. It's even clearer than when he hears it through his earpiece during runtime, which is always so intimate in its own way. It almost sounds like he's—

"I'm here. I'm right here, I don't know if you can hear me, but I'm here, and I'm so glad you're here too. God, you scared the hell out of me."

Warm pressure on his hand, someone holding it. That was real too. That wasn't a dream. It couldn't be, not when their hands fit together this perfectly like they always do. He could feel Jay's long fingers and slight calluses and touching is unmistakable as seeing, impossible to replicate or fake. It was him.

"But you did the right thing, smashing your monitor, I know why you did that now. You were trying to keep him from tracing me."

Regan forced his aching eyes open. At first he saw nothing but a blurry sea of white, painful, it hurt just to have them open a crack. His eyes drifted down and there's a dark, just as blurry shape beside him. He couldn't see a face but he didn't need to.

"And you tried to warn me—what you said. 'Blood in the water.' I got the message, Regan. I heard you, and you're safe now, and I'm right here. I'm not going anywhere. And neither are you. You hear me? You're not. I... I called Stefanos. He's coming back early. The FireRunner should make it home by..."

Jay was still talking but Regan couldn't understand the words anymore. Still, he tried to answer. He tried to say how grateful he is that Jay's not only alive and safe but here with him. *They made it. They're still together and nothing is going to separate them ever again.* But he couldn't form words, his face was still numb and his tongue wouldn't work, it felt swollen, too big for his mouth.

He couldn't even keep his eyes open, so he let them relax and close, and the second they were shut, he was falling again, but not before he told his hand to squeeze back. Before he knew if he actually did or not, he was gone.

The next thing Regan saw and heard, he was sure wasn't a hallucination. It had to be real. Too bright and painful to be anything but real. His face was still numb and his entire body felt like it was made of lead and anchored to the ocean floor. Waves of painful pins and needles swept through his arms and legs, like poison coursing through his veins. Considering everything he'd been through, that might not be far from the truth.

"BP's coming down now. One-forty over ninety-six," someone said, or that's what he thought they said; the words were garbled and sounded like he was underwater. Or maybe they were. "Out of crisis territory now, but still higher than I'd like. He should spike again in about an hour if the frequency stays consistent."

Rowan's voice, he realized, and the wave of relief that swept over him was so profound he almost sank back into unconsciousness again. His traumatized brain had told him so convincingly that they were gone, that they'd never met, that they'd been taken away from one another and would never see each other again. But he could see Rowan now. His vision still swam and everything was too bright but he could make out the red-gold waves and curls of their hair, the curved, ridged black of one horn. They weren't looking at him, and didn't seem to have noticed he'd opened his eyes.

"At least it seems like they're getting further apart," they said in a too-calm voice, a cadence much smoother and precise than their usual one. It didn't sound right. It didn't sound like them. "I wish we knew how much Chrysedrine they gave him. We could be looking at days, a week, or longer depending on the dosage."

Regan knew what they were doing, he realized with a pang of anxiety. He'd seen and heard this before. This was the voice Rowan used when they were talking about—but not to—a patient in danger, someone too far gone to hear. The mask they put on in a crisis, the one that took them a million miles away. Far from Regan, where he was scared and hurting and might be dying, he definitely felt like it, and if he was dying, he didn't want the last thing he saw to be that mask. He wanted *Rowan*.

He reached out weakly and by some miracle caught Rowan's hand as they passed by. They froze, entire body going rigid, stopping mid-sentence. It didn't even look like they were breathing as they turned to face him, Tartarus-black eyes wide.

"You're here," he whispered, sandpaper throat burning and so thick he could barely get the words out. But they were important words. He was vaguely aware that he'd heard them somewhere before. Jay said the same thing when he was here, and he wasn't here anymore, leaving an aching absence, but Rowan was, and Regan had never been so relieved.

They didn't answer or move, but as he watched, tears spilled from their eyes. Why were they crying? What made them hurt like this? Even in his semiconscious state Regan had the terrible feeling that it was because of him, and the strange fear that had plagued his fever dreams came back with a vengeance. Rowan gone, disappeared, never having come into his life at all. He wouldn't know them to miss them, but the thought made his stomach feel hollow anyway. But it wasn't real. He was looking right at them, and life still made sense.

"You're here," he murmured to cement the fact, sinking deep into relief like a warm bath. Even if Rowan didn't say a word, just stared at him, that was better than anything he'd feared. His bad dreams had been just that, dreams brought on by Chrysedrine's physical and psychological ravages. This was real, and even if this reality hurt, he'd take it over the one he dreaded. "You're fine, Rowan. You're here with me. Zilch didn't do it."

"What?" Now Rowan spoke at last, voice a dry whisper that sounded brittle, near breaking.

"They didn't do it," Regan said, a rare and beautiful clarity cutting through his murky consciousness. If he could only know one thing for sure, let it be this. "They didn't kill you. You're fine."

He let out a long, deep sigh—then heard a strange noise, something between a gasp and a startled word. It didn't come from Rowan; they were still staring at him but not crying anymore, or smiling. Instead, they looked confused and curious—the mask was back—as if he'd said something very strange instead of the simplest, purest fact in the world. Rowan started talking again, but they were just more words he couldn't understand. Another voice replied, but by the time Regan recognized it— *Zilch! Zilch is here!*—he was falling again.

🔥

He falls back into darkness but Zilch is still there, always there, always will be, the one who'd taken him by the hand and led him safely away from SkEye's searchlights, stayed beside him all these years, never leaving him now. Long arms and soft black cloth have always been around him, protecting him from everything outside it that wants to hurt him, and there are many things that do. The world might change around him (who outside Parole would even recognize this place as being on Earth?), rivers vanish and fire devours, stars disappear and smoke fills the air, but there's always been enough air in his lungs while they're together.

He has a whole conversation with Jay that he can't remember now, even if he can remember exactly what they were talking about before this all started— favorite superpowers, what would you pick? Regan would stay exactly who he is right now, he'd be the same, he likes who he is, he loves his life, it's strange but it's his and it took him long enough to get here—and how Jay would pick being able to do the last five seconds over. It feels like that now, time repeating, endless nights with his voice in Regan's ear, endless reunions after victory, endless kisses, endless hours together in a messy bed with smooth black hair falling around him, pooling like liquid, smelling like the man he loves (with his entire heart, endlessly) and making every bit of stubborn tension in Regan's body fade. Endless moments in this small, cozy-dark room lit by computer screens' glows and filled with white-noise fans and cat purrs. Maybe it's the lizard in him, loving this cool, dark place, but he loves the man who lives in it even more, and how he and everything else here is safe, safe, safe.

Ash carries him home. Time blends together and he does it right now, the way he's done it before, maybe yesterday or a year ago. Parole's Reaper always kept him safe and sound and Regan still almost laughs remembering that's what they call Ash. It's people who don't know him who say that, because even if they mean it in a grateful, awed way, even if the Reaper is a protective and comforting figure here in this strange fiery city, it still doesn't fit his exuberant, pick-you-up-off-the-ground hugs and terrible puns he laughs at himself, and the happy dogs who follow him around knowing he's the softest touch in Parole. And his touch is one of the softest, his large hands, missing a finger, that have brought death to so many SkEye soldiers and mercy to doomed runners—they've only ever been warm and gentle to little girls and dog ears and scared lizard boys, and he almost feels them, even if they're not real, Regan thanks the deep-buried sense memory that brings them to life now.

More faces and hands and voices and laughs float through his head, or he floats through them. It feels like he's on a carousel that's spinning too fast, and every time he turns around there's someone new to miss and love and hope he gets to see again.

Annie clinging to his leg and begging him not to go, once she was old enough to understand runtimes were dangerous, but too young not to cry at the thought of him not coming home. So small, so brave, going to do such amazing things and he can't wait to tell her how proud he is to see them all.

Radio Angel's voice in his earpiece, sweet and comforting and one of the last bright spots left in this scorched place.

The smooth black sheen on Celeste's visor, her silver stars that mean a situation really is serious, but it isn't over, it's never over once she gets started.

Golden, humming gyroscope eyes that flash like shards of glass in the sun when Stefanos smiles and makes him feel like this isn't the end, it's the beginning of an adventure and all Regan can do is hold onto the feeling of being wonderfully bear-hug crushed against his broad chest, hearing the whir of machinery under his laugh, and try to believe him.

And Rowan. Not dead, not gone, warm and safe in his arms as he's always been safe in theirs. Understanding him without words, loving him without pressure or expectations, kissing him without pretense or hesitation, telling him without question that this is real, this is forever. This is a pair of gentle hands that help him dress for a run, attaching vitals monitors and buckling a knife holster around his thigh, the same hands that will take it all off when he comes home from an exhausting, deadly night. A long, quiet day spent wrapped around each other, sleeping and waking for slow, lazy kisses, a warmth and sense of calm that quells the fever and panic in him. A dear, desperate wish for a future with more days like that, and even more nights.

Regan tries to hang onto these memories and hopes—all of them, any of them—but they slip through his fingers not like sand, but the water Parole has craved since it was banished from the rest of the world.

He's falling again, falling away from sight and sound and recognition and the people he loves, all of them, they're all getting so far away now, and he doesn't know where he's falling or what will happen when he hits the ground, only that he's falling faster all the time.

"Hey, Regan," Stefanos said in a low voice, a metallic-sounding whir under each word. He leaned forward in his chair to speak quietly in Regan's ear, synthetic elbows resting on his equally artificial knees, golden eyes moving in slow, constant, multi-geared rotations. "Not sure how much of this you can hear, but I know if that was me lying there, I'd want people to talk to me, just in case. It'd get really boring otherwise."

He let out a short, also slightly metallic-sounding laugh, but it died quickly.

"Definitely hasn't been boring out here though. Jay called me. Took a little wrangling, but the FireRunner made it home. I know Aliyah will be glad to see you when you wake up... and Jay's here now too. He's just outside. He'll see when you when you wake up. It's hard for him to see you like this, you know? You know why. But he can't stay away either, and neither will I. Not until you're on the other side of this."

Stefanos sat back and watched Regan breathe for a few seconds, and the occasional twitches of his frill. Lizard boy was dreaming something, he thought. Hopefully good dreams.

"Gave us a scare, that's for sure," he continued. "But it's not your fault. This isn't on you, none of it. It's on... well, you know who's fault it is. And so do we, don't worry about that. We know what he did. And we need *you* to know that he's not going to get away with it. And he's never going to do it again. Not to you. Never again."

Regan didn't answer, of course. But he did move slightly, and Stefanos' electric heart leaped—until he saw that Regan's eyes remained tightly shut, and this was no conscious motion. He was shaking, arms twitching, small movements getting bigger and more violent with every second.

"Rowan," Stefanos said in an only slightly louder voice, keeping it as calm as possible.

"He's crashing again," Rowan said briskly, rushing in and putting their hands on Regan's shoulders to keep him from jolting himself right off the bed. Stefanos had only seen them in their element—emergency medical, crisis, triage—a few times, thankfully. Still, it was amazing how fast they snapped into action, seeming hyperaware but not panicked, and entirely present in this immediate, terrifying moment. "Find Zilch! Get them back here, now!"

"On it," Stefanos said, throwing open the door where Jay stood outside in the hall, facing away from the door but turning quickly around as it opened. Stefanos carefully arranged his large frame between Jay and the doorway, hopefully blocking the worst of it from view. "Jay, where'd Zilch go?"

"I, I, uh, they went to find Annie," Jay stammered, obviously startled and his exhaustion quickly ramping back up to fear. That was bad enough. If it got worse than this, Stefanos thought, if the worst happened, Jay shouldn't be here to see it. So he wouldn't.

"Get them back here, tell them Regan needs them," Stefanos said, gently steering Jay down the hall and away from Regan's room. "Go find—"

"Zilch," Rowan said late on the morning of the third day.

Zilch didn't exactly sleep, but they could get pretty deep down into a trancelike state. Once Regan stabilized again—soon after Zilch returned, maybe there really was something to believing unconscious patients were still partly aware—they spent more and more time staring, unblinking and unmoving into the middle distance, unnaturally still without even the hint of breath or anything else that suggested life. Until Rowan's voice shook them from their reverie and drew their attention back to the present.

"Yes?" they asked, eyes on Rowan, who was staring in turn at Regan, expression a studied blank, unreadable even to Zilch. They'd had trouble reading Rowan at all in the past few days; Zilch had seen their medical-professional pokerface at work before, but never thought they'd be on the receiving end. That, like so many other things right now, felt wrong.

"Look at him," Rowan said with a little nod toward Regan, who seemed to lie calmer in bed, shakes having subsided once the last wave was over. "How does he look to you?"

Zilch studied Regan's face—a healthier, more saturated green now, free of tension. If Zilch hadn't been witness to the past three days, they'd think he was just sleeping, escaping from pain and worry the way he didn't do nearly enough. His chest rose and fall regularly, and the rest of him remained still, not so much as a twitch in any of his fingers.

"Better," Zilch said, tentative, hopeful but ready to be proven wrong.

"That's because I think he is," Rowan said, voice hushed and filled with something that sounded caught between disbelief and awe, something Zilch rarely heard from them. "No fever. Blood pressure and heart are... normal. Normal and holding for a few minutes now."

"That's a good thing, isn't it?" Zilch asked, not ready to trust entirely, but unable to help the hope surging up inside them. Hope was possible to restrain, but not to ignore.

"He made it," Rowan said, and now Zilch did see some raw, undisguised emotion on their face: complete shock and an incredulity that made their disembodied heart ache. How close had Regan come to death if Rowan was this surprised he'd survived? "He'll wake up hurting, but he'll wake up. He's not going to die."

Then Rowan swayed, legs shaking like they wouldn't support them anymore, and before Zilch could move to catch them, fell into the chair next to Regan. Their only break in this nightmare had been the middle of the second day, when Zilch was able to convince them to nap on the only other bed in the room. They hadn't entertained any suggestions of another rest since, ready to push themself until they dropped, and the consequences showed themselves now.

Rowan slumped forward until their head and forearms lay on Regan's bed, not on his chest but near it, and clinging to his hand. Zilch watched their shoulders shake, watched them finally give in to the weight of pain and horror they'd suppressed for three days, and the even more powerful force of relief.

"Rowan," Zilch said quietly from behind them, still resisting their automatic urge to touch their shoulder, stroke their soft, curly hair. When Rowan looked up at the gentle sound of their name, their face was red, tears spilling from their black eyes and leaving wet stains on Regan's sheets. Zilch stepped hesitantly toward them and tentatively raised one hand, carefully watching their face. "Can I...?"

"Yes!" Rowan cried, reaching out toward Zilch and pulling them close, wrapping one arm around their waist and leaving more tears on their black, ragged top layer, which Zilch didn't mind at all. "Yes, please touch me, talk to me, say whatever you need to say now—I'm sorry I couldn't handle it before. I just couldn't..."

"I know," Zilch said, reaching up to stroke Rowan's face and hair now, finding both soft as ever and making their touch soft to match. "You did the right thing. You did good."

"I..." Rowan couldn't seem to get words out anymore, or find them. Their attempt just became a sob, and they broke down again, still holding tight onto Zilch with one hand, and Regan with the other.

"You did good." Zilch repeated quietly, as Rowan fell forward again to collapse onto Regan's bed, shaking and exhausted and completely weak. They said it a few more times, because each time made Rowan shudder and release more tension. There was so much built up inside them, all of it painful, and Zilch couldn't stand to let a single bit remain. The two of them stayed like that for several minutes, Rowan crying out their fear and pain and buried love, Zilch murmuring quiet words of comfort, stroking the back of their head, eyes on Regan's healthier-colored, finally serene sleeping face.

"Will you be all right for a minute?" Zilch asked at last, after Rowan's shaking sobs subsided and they raised their head, starting to wipe off their face.

"More or less," they said with a little sigh that neared embarrassment, but would never be fully so, not between the three of them. Zilch would be hard pressed to say when they'd seen each other worse off, but in eight years, there had to be another time. "I don't think any of us will be all right for a while, but I'm so much better than I was. And so is he." They turned from where they'd been fondly looking at Regan to give Zilch a questioning look as they nodded and took a step toward the door. "Where are you going?"

"Ash promised Annie she could see him as soon as he was stable," Zilch said. "And I know he'll want to too. And Jay. He should see Regan doing better than last time he was here."

"Okay," Rowan said, nodding and looking a little more steady, but still exhausted. "I think that's fine. He needs to sleep, but if I remember post-withdrawal correctly, he'll be out for another day or two at least, and nothing has much chance of waking him up. And seeing him stable should do them all a lot of good. It certainly did me."

"Good," Zilch said, opening the door and looking back on the threshold, at both of them, Regan breathing easily and Rowan lowering their head back down onto his bed. None of them were as they should be yet, their broken pieces not begun to fit back together, but they would. They always did when the three of them were together. Zilch wouldn't rest until they were. "I'll be back soon."

Regan was still sleeping peacefully a few hours later. And now, so was Annie, in the other bed. The second she heard the good news, she'd burst into Regan's room, took one look at him in the bed, and broke down crying almost as hard as Rowan had. When she was done, she refused to leave, and neither Rowan or Zilch could find it in themselves to argue with her.

She almost hadn't been the only one to fall asleep in here. Jay had been shaky and weak on his feet, all dark circles and coffee jitters, looking like he hadn't slept at all in the past three days—or longer. Seeing Regan alive, if not completely well, had struck him speechless in the way nothing else did. He'd stayed with Regan for as long as he could without collapsing from exhaustion, trying to form words and failing, dissolving into incoherent emotional noises and finally stopping his attempts in favor of sitting still and just being with him.

Ash took Jay home when he did fall asleep upright for a second, which he vehemently denied. But he did see the sense of it—Jay might still be a mess, but *CyborJ* had responsibilities, and who knew what peril the city had fallen into without him? He needed to sleep and get back to work. Jay didn't do well with nothing to focus on except fear, and nothing to do with himself besides worry.

Neither did Ash, but he was much more likely to actually be able to sleep. In here, maybe, when he came back to check on Annie. It was a small room, with only two beds, but they were a small, strange, resourceful family and they'd figure something out.

"I'm sorry, again," Rowan said quietly to Zilch, just now starting to clean up the mess that had accumulated over the past days. Giving Regan a clean change of sheets would be next, but they'd need Zilch's help for that. Otherwise, they had a system. "For how I was before. So detached and... cold."

"You had to stay calm," Zilch said, one gray patchwork hand gently resting on Regan's chest, feeling it rise and fall, feeling the finally-steady heartbeat within. Understanding, even if detaching like that wasn't something they'd ever be able to do themself. "You can't function if you're panicking. If you think someone you love is dying. Nothing else exists."

"Yes, exactly," Rowan said with a slight sag of their shoulders—clear further relief at Zilch's understanding. "It was too much, if I started to feel it, I'd freeze when he needed me most, and for that... he couldn't be Regan. He couldn't be our sweet boy." Their voice broke and they were silent for a moment, and very still. When they continued, they'd recovered some, words still raw but steadier. "And you couldn't be *you* watching this, and I couldn't even be me. It all had to be happening to someone else, somewhere else."

Now Rowan stopped moving completely, staring at Zilch and Regan, or maybe past them, toward other, less happy possibilities. Zilch could pretty well guess the kind of less-favorable outcome they were seeing. Regan lying even more still than he was now, not breathing and never to wake up. The two of them holding each other and his too-cool body while the world fell apart around and inside them, all of them falling into irreparable pieces no matter how tightly they clung to one another. The emptiness that would suck all the air out of the room, Zilch's promises to the contrary turning them into a liar, because without Regan there would never be enough air, not in the entire world.

"But it wasn't just that," Rowan said, and while their voice didn't shake anymore, there was something else Zilch didn't like any better. Guilt, loud and clear and painful. "I was trying to make myself numb so it wouldn't hurt... as much. When he died."

Again Zilch wanted nothing more than to wrap their arms around Rowan, and at any other time, that would have been the right thing without question. They'd all been comfortably tactile with each other since their beginning, finding comfort in each others' bodies and presence, and touch came as easily as breathing. But Rowan was clearly still trying to find their footing after this ordeal, when breathing had been difficult indeed, and Zilch would hold back until expressly invited. They stayed where they were, hand on Regan's chest, feeling it rise and fall, though they were no longer afraid he'd slip away the second they let go.

"He *didn't* die." Zilch looked at them with love in their mismatched eyes and gratitude in their heart, floating elsewhere in this building, still safe in its jar. Safe every moment Regan's heart beat too. "Because of you. You did that."

"Believe me, I had very little to do with it," Rowan said with a slight scoff—that was good, even self-deprecating laughter was a step forward. "It was all him." They paused then, turned a strange, considering look toward Zilch, seeming to ponder them with a flicker of realization—or maybe suspicion.

Zilch's blood couldn't really run cold, but they still felt a stab of fear, and found it impossible to meet Rowan's suddenly speculative, probing eyes. Even all black, there was no mistaking their curiosity.

"I should have told you before," Zilch blurted, looking at the floor between their differently-sized feet and holding onto Regan's hand just a bit tighter.

"Told me what?" Rowan asked, sounding confused—but it was too late. They had to know. If they didn't yet, they would now.

"What Regan said. About you being alive. And me not killing you." Zilch made themselves say the words. If they could taste, these would be bitter, like ashes, but holding them inside any longer would be worse still.

After everything they'd been through—after how close they'd come to losing Regan—how could Zilch keep silent a moment longer? How could they risk never getting another chance?

"What he said?" Zilch looked up to see Rowan looking thoroughly confused, and for the first time thought they may have miscalculated. "I thought that was all withdrawal hallucination word salad. People always say bizarre things when they're going through that. Do you mean that was actually...?"

They must have seen the despairing look on Zilch's face, because their confusion was soon replaced by serious, earnest openness that any other time might have been reassuring. Now, this, along with any other kindness Rowan might conceivably do them, would only make everything worse.

"I'm listening." Rowan sat down next to Regan's bed in the chair they'd collapsed into before, much more calmly now, which couldn't be said for Zilch. They held absolutely still, fighting the urge to run, pretend this had never happened, and that their lives could continue the way they always had until this point. As if everything wasn't about to be ruined forever.

"The first time I saw you," Zilch began at last, and now a slight smile did actually pull at the corner of their stitched mouth. It was a strange memory to hold dear, even wrong to be so fond of it, but they couldn't help it, and after eight years they'd stopped trying. "I'll never forget it."

"Me neither," Rowan said with an answering soft smile. "Seeing you and Regan come in here—"

"No. That's when we *met*," Zilch cut in, voice even flatter than usual. They couldn't look at Rowan anymore. "The first time I *saw* you was before then. A day earlier. You were on the library roof."

"I used to love it there," Rowan said, faltering a little but not running away yet, at least. "We had the helicopter surveillance patterns memorized, and there used to be a five minute break on Thursday evenings. I'd go up there to look outside, up at the sky, what you can see. Look around at the place. It was foolish, I know, but it was only for a few minutes every week or so. Spending my whole life in the library or its basement could get a little..." they stopped, and Zilch didn't need to look up to feel their staring eyes. "How did you know that?"

"Because I was on the next roof. Watching you. Through a rifle's scope."

Rowan's mouth dropped open but they didn't interrupt. They held perfectly still.

"It was an assignment," Zilch continued, numb. "From Turret. He wanted the library. But they couldn't get in, it was airtight."

"Ash always made sure of that," Rowan said a little faintly, and Zilch could imagine their pensive, brow-furrowed Puzzling It Out expression, the one they got while pondering the latest riddle of survival in Parole. "We didn't even know for sure if they knew..."

"They knew. SkEye knew even back then that the library was a resistance center. They knew what you looked like. And I was their best. I waited on that rooftop for days, watching for the next time you popped your head out."

It was the truth. But it wasn't the whole truth. Zilch left out the part about how they'd gotten that information, how they'd learned about the rooftop activity in the first place. They were the assassin, but not the source. Regan was always the scout. But Zilch couldn't acknowledge that in words, not with him lying here unable to defend himself.

"So what happened?" Rowan asked, remarkably calmly given the circumstances, Zilch thought. They were being remarkably calm about all of this, actually. It didn't quite feel like their professional mask, but it wasn't what Zilch had expected either. "You obviously didn't kill me. Which I know is... unusual. From what they made you do."

"Unusual?" Zilch smiled sadly, an ache seeming to radiate from their disembodied heart all the way through their entire being, all their disparate parts united in shame. "You were the first. Every single other target I was assigned, taken out with precision and ease."

Rowan shivered audibly, and Zilch's heart constricted now as well as ached. "So then—why? What made me any different? You didn't love me then. You didn't even *know* me."

Slowly, Zilch raised their head to look not at Rowan, but across the room to the other bed, where Annie still slept peacefully. A wonderful thing to keep their eyes on through this difficult conversation with Rowan, the one they could only hope wouldn't be their last.

"Her. She followed you up there. Must have been... ten? Ran right up to you. You picked her up."

"She was such a tiny thing," Rowan said, sounding faraway. Maybe wistful, maybe dissociating again, the way Zilch knew they had been the whole time Regan was in danger. "She hit a growth spurt right after that. That's one of the last times I could..."

"And then Ash was there," Zilch made themselves continue. "Followed her up, got the two of you back inside, but he was laughing. I could hear it from where I was."

"I remember that day," Rowan said, voice dropping to just above a whisper. They were understanding now, Zilch thought. Really understanding. In this case, understanding may lead to the end of everything they held dear. But it still needed to happen. "I remember what I thought, looking at the sky. That it had been quiet that week. Peaceful. That even in Parole, you could still find some happiness. And then, yes, Annie and Ash were there, and just for a moment, it felt like... like we weren't here. Like everything was ordinary, and we were just another family. I felt so lucky." Their smile faded as they focused back on Zilch. "I suppose I was. More than I knew."

"As SkEye's Operative Zero, I had many targets. No," Zilch amended, eyes narrowing, cold fury aimed entirely inward. "I've *killed many people*. Innocents, probably. Definitely. That's the truth of it. But never one holding a little girl. Not a family."

Rowan didn't reply. And for a while, Zilch didn't speak either, just let their hand slip from its perch on Regan's chest to his hand, clutching it. When they continued at last, they still couldn't look up, directing their words to the floor and holding onto Regan's hand like now they were the one who might slip away without it.

"It wasn't a good deed," they said. "Just not killing someone is nothing to applaud. But it was something SkEye would have punished, severely. They knew what I did. That I'd spared you. Regan—*Chimera*—

already had too many strikes against him. And they'd have punished him anyway, to punish me. It was the only way to get to Zero and they knew it. They would have killed him. Or much worse. But I did it anyway. I was done. Both of us were. They had children there, Rowan. Teenagers, girls and boys, locked in cages. Not that much older than... than Annie. We'd been planning for months to get them out. But seeing her, that's when it all came together. We had to go."

"Sounds like we were the final straw," Rowan said quietly, tone unreadable. Still, Zilch wouldn't allow themself to look at Rowan's face. That would come too close to excusing what they'd done, begging for mercy they didn't come close to deserving.

Zilch's voice was a bone-dry rasp by now, every word an effort to get out. "I had no idea. Seeing the three of you then. How important you would be to me. To both of us." Their eyes slipped shut, and they let their head hang lower. It was done. "I am so, so sorry, Rowan."

Again, no reply. Silence stretched between them, and every second hurt. But when Rowan finally broke it, their words were the last ones Zilch had expected or dreaded for all these years.

"Thank you."

"Don't *thank* me," Zilch said, looking up at last, horrified by the very thought. They stared at Rowan, who was looking back with tears in their black eyes. Not quite breaking down, but from the looks of it, just barely. At that sight, Zilch's heart, though safe in its jar, felt like it would fall apart into too many pieces to ever repair. "Shout at me. Hate me, for keeping this from you all these years. Basing everything we have on a lie—"

"No," Rowan cut in with a shake of their head Zilch knew took more effort than for most people, with their heavy horns to contend with. Apparently this was important enough to warrant it. "No, not a lie. This was..."

Rowan fell silent again, eyes shut and both hands going to rub their eyes, drag down their face. Then, without speaking, they stood up. Silently walked the few steps around Regan's bed to where Zilch waited ready for anything. Any punishment, any accusation, any horrified pain at their betrayal that had poisoned eight otherwise wonderful, life-changing, life-affirming years. Everything they had, tainted. Zilch was ready to walk out the door, the way they had been the moment they'd come here with Regan. Secure a safe place for him here, he was innocent, that was the one good thing Zero had been able to do. He deserved a chance at a new life. If Zero had been forced to leave eight years ago, then so be it. If Zilch had to do the same now, how was it any different?

Then Rowan's arms were around their neck, their lips pressed against Zilch's temple. They didn't move when a long shudder swept through Zilch's entire body, a strange, emotional-physical reaction they thought their sewn-together form had long since left behind, but here it was. Zilch shook. Almost as hard as Regan caught in the throes of withdrawal. Shook so hard they couldn't be sure they were all in one piece, only knowing they must be, because Rowan was still holding them. Holding them together.

"I could have killed you," Zilch whispered, tentatively reaching up to curl their arms loosely around Rowan's soft waist, still not quite convinced they wouldn't pull away. Zilch didn't weep tears; they'd lost that capacity for certain. But they could still cry. Now they shook even harder, heaving in violent, dry sobs, face buried in Rowan's shoulder for once. How many times had their positions been reversed? How many times, whenever they'd held or kissed or touched Rowan at all, had Zilch felt like an undeserving liar?

"You didn't kill me," Rowan said, a hand on the back of their head, stroking their patchy hair and then just resting there.

"I could have destroyed everything before I even met you. Our whole family."

"You *didn't*. You saved us, you joined us. You made it complete."

"I still should have told you before," Zilch insisted, still almost wanting Rowan's anger by this point, that righteous and fiery fury that they'd seen only a few times, but remained in awe of. Wanting their condemnation, anything but this *acceptance* they didn't have the first idea how to handle. How to endure. Rowan must have misunderstood somehow. Why else would any of this be happening? "Long before. When you first let us stay here, I should have told you what I almost did. But I couldn't risk us being kicked out. Regan wouldn't have survived."

"I know." From the way Rowan's tufted chin rested on Zilch's head now, they had to be looking back at Regan. Remembering that first day? Being terrified of how easily it could have gone differently? Going weak with relief that he was still here, they were all still together right now?

Like Zilch, everything all at once?

"And then too much time had passed," Zilch continued, speaking much faster than their usual halting cadence. Now that they'd started explaining, found the words after years of silence, they found it hard to stop. "I didn't know how—and then, you and Regan. And then, you and *me*." Not entirely intentionally, they held Rowan a little tighter. "And by then—it would have ruined everything. Everything we had and fought for since we left SkEye with nothing. I couldn't..."

Zilch trailed off, words finally failing, and Rowan held them while they shook some more and muffled their dry sobs in Rowan's shirt, painfully aware of both Regan and Annie sleeping nearby, how precious their sleep was, and how completely Zilch would be incapable of explaining if they woke up and asked what was happening.

"Thank you for telling me now," Rowan said at last, voice soft and faraway-sounding again, but with none of the blame or judgement Zilch so easily expected and richly deserved. How?

"If this is... too much..." Zilch said, their own voice still a painful rasp. "I understand. But it's not Regan's fault. He wanted me to tell you years ago. I made him swear not to. I would when I was ready, and then I was just—never ready. I'm sorry. Please let him stay."

"Let him—*Zilch!*" Rowan almost laughed, and Zilch almost collapsed with combined relief and regret. "Regan isn't going anywhere. Including out of this room, not for several days at least. And neither are you. Too much?" Rowan repeated, giving another shake of their head—but this time, against all reason and justice, they were smiling. "I think all of our definitions of 'too much' have shifted, along with the rest of this place. You're right, this is... a lot to take in."

Rowan paused, voice sobering a bit. So they did feel something besides gratitude and forgiveness, Zilch thought, with less fear than they'd anticipated, and much more relief. Good. This should give them pause. They should think long and hard about trusting Zilch—*Zero*—or letting them into their life, or their heart. Even if they already had. Even if Ash had too, and Annie, even if Zilch and Regan had found a home here, and were truly happy in a world full of impossible things, where that simple happiness seemed the most impossible. They had to know how much blood stained Zilch's hands, no matter how many times Rowan had lovingly replaced them.

"And yes, it'll take a while for me to process everything," Rowan continued after a bit. But they still didn't sound angry, or hurt beyond healing, and it was still *them*. Not their detached doctor mask; this was Rowan who still had their arms around Zilch and showed no signs of leaving. "But you don't have to worry. You never have to worry about not having a place here, or me not loving you. I don't care what you did then, or what you do now—some things will never happen, not even in Parole."

Zilch just held onto them for a while longer, before slowly looking up into their face again. Rowan's eyes were dry now, and even if they were never the easiest to read, Zilch saw the mix of emotions in their face easily enough, the love and pain, certainty and worry. Zilch certainly felt all of that themself. And relief—like when Regan had taken his first smooth breath, relief palpable and overpowering. But most of all, Zilch just felt bewildered.

"How can this not change anything?"

"Of course it changes things," Rowan said easily, and for a moment all of Zilch's terror came roaring back.

But Rowan seemed to sense this, because then their hand was on Zilch's cheek, gently turning their face back up when they'd let their head drop again. "It changes things because now I know that on top of all the other times you've saved us, there's one more. I know even better what you'd do to protect Regan. And me. *Us*. Strangers you didn't even know. I know even better what our life means to you, and what you risked to get it."

They broke into a smile then, their first real one since Regan's fever broke. All at once, Zilch could breathe.

"I was right," Rowan sighed, fatigue showing on their round face for the first time in days. They leaned more heavily against Zilch, who didn't move an inch. They never did. "Like I said—I am luckier than I ever knew."

"I wanted this," Zilch said, looking up at Rowan with the beginnings of hope, that most beautiful and elusive thing that sometimes came with feathers, or horns, or shining green scales. Slowly, they raised one hand to touch Rowan's face like making sure they were real—and they immediately demonstrated that they were, catching Zilch's hand in theirs and pressing a kiss to their fingertips. "Not just since leaving SkEye. Since Chrysedrine. Even longer, before any of this happened. Before

Parole happened. I wanted a family. I wanted *you*, before I ever saw you. Maybe that's why I stopped. I don't know. I just know that I'm so glad to be here."

"Me too," Rowan said, and this at least, Zilch had no trouble believing. Then they were both looking at Regan again, as one, without words. "And, God... I'm glad *he's* here."

Rowan put one hand on Regan's bed then, and Zilch could still read them easily enough to know they were contemplating climbing into bed with him, as they'd done so many times before. But not on a bed this small, and not when Regan had just been battered harder and more brutally than anything he'd suffered in his already-traumatic life. Worse than they could even know, thanks to the Chrysedrine, Zilch remembered with a kind of dark resolution. Sharpe would pay. But for now, Zilch just held out one arm and waved down at themself, an invitation Rowan immediately took, settling down in their arms and keeping their eyes on the rise and fall of Regan's chest.

"You've never seen someone make it through a second withdrawal before?" Zilch asked after a while, voice still dry but much closer to normal than it had been.

"Never. I have no idea how he did it," Rowan said, reaching up to run their thumb over Regan's cheekbone, smiling when he shifted his head just a little to lean into their touch. "He's stronger than I ever knew. I should really stop being surprised by now."

The two of them lapsed into another silence, much more comfortable than Zilch would have thought possible after only one of the two momentous things that had just happened; Regan's survival, and the survival of their bond. Their joined lives, their triad, their foundation so much stronger than Parole's crumbling streets.

"This can't happen again," Rowan said after another, longer pause. They didn't sound faraway anymore, instead more determined, resolved. It was a promise as much as a warning, Zilch thought. And they always trusted Rowan's promises. "It won't matter how strong he is if it does. That I do know."

"It won't," Zilch swore, pulling Rowan a little closer. Regan was alive, he'd wake up safe if not yet healthy, and Zilch would tell him there would be no more secrets, no more lies, even lies of omission. They'd all have more time. More time together, alive and safe and in each others' arms.

There was no way of knowing what time it was in this small room, insulated and isolated from the chaos outside. But now, the sun might come out again, beyond the barrier overhead. The moon and stars would rise, present and eternal even hidden behind smoke and searchlights. Now the air was clear.

Different People

EIGHT YEARS BEFORE CHAMELEON MOON

The first time Regan says the words, he thinks he's ready. No, knows it. Knows it the way he knows there's a barrier above and a newly lit fire below. The way death is a near and sure thing in Parole, even if taxes aren't—or weather, or fresh air, or freedom, or nights free of searchlights and sirens. He knows it like he knows he needs to escape, like he knows the world keeps turning outside, going on without them, forgetting everyone imprisoned here. The way he knows everyone in Parole is on their own, but not alone, not anymore.

The knowledge terrifies him, and the words scare him even more,

but he also can't keep them inside for another minute, or he might just burst into flame himself.

"Rowan, I think I—I'm in love with you."

"Regan…" they say back, and they're so patient, voice so gentle that he *knows* immediately, and his heart sinks. "This happens all the time. Firefighters, EMTs, search and rescue crews. They save peoples' lives, and emotions are running so high, adrenaline and desperation, and all of these powerful feelings get focused on the person who saved—"

"No, no, that's not what this is. This is different. I really have… feelings for you. Good ones. They're real."

"I'm not saying they aren't. In fact, I'm sure they are. Everything you feel is 'real,' for the circumstances. But this might not be as… organic, as it might have been, if we hadn't met the way we did."

"…So you're saying you don't feel the same way about me?"

He almost fades away right there. Feels the cold shiver as he starts to turn invisible. At least Chrysedrine had given him the ability to disappear whenever he wanted, and he wants nothing more right now. But Rowan's hand reaches out and takes his while it's still half-visible, and he stops, caught between hope and the reason it was called a 'crush.'

"I'm saying wait. If these feelings are real, in the way you mean, they'll still be here. If not, I don't want you to feel bad. I'm glad you're in my life, Regan. So glad."

"Okay. Okay, yeah. You're probably right. You usually are."

"Just give it time. You're still healing. Let yourself have some time to breathe."

"Yeah. Um... don't go anywhere, okay?"

"Don't worry, I'm not going anywhere. And neither are you."

The second time he tells them, it's nine months later. He's pressed against their side and half-awake, half still in the kind of lazy dream he only seemed to have when sleeping with Rowan—actually sleeping, a wonderful habit they'd fallen into after he'd fallen asleep on them as they read together in his beanbag chair nest, and Rowan hadn't moved until he woke up. They hadn't spoken about it; they hadn't needed to. They still don't.

"Rowan."

"Hmm?" They sound half-asleep too.

"I... there's something..." Words aren't forming. He's just awake enough to know that he should be wracked with anxiety, terrified—but apparently just asleep enough not to be. He isn't afraid, and any other time, that alone might have frightened him.

"What is it?" Rowan asks, sounding a little clearer. He feels more than sees them look down at him, their arm curling a little tighter around his waist, relaxing him further.

"Just hear me out," he says, adrenaline shaking him the rest of the way awake. Rowan doesn't interrupt, so he keeps going as his heart starts to pound. "I know what I said before—and how you said the feelings are real, but they might not be right. And you were right, but I was right too. Just not for the right reasons."

"Regan... what are we talking about?" They definitely sound awake now, but obviously not comprehending. Regan swallows and takes a breath, and then the plunge.

"When I first woke up, out of withdrawal, I didn't know you. I thought I loved you, because you were a good person who was nice to me, and saved my life. But it wasn't real love, it couldn't be, I know that now. And I know that this time is different. Because *I'm* different, but I feel the same way."

And he is different—an entirely different person, in some ways. It hasn't even been a year but they've adapted. Regan's learned that there might be an unseeing world outside of Parole, but even within its barrier, there was a whole new world he'd never imagined. He had a place that wasn't a SkEye facility full of bright lights and cold floors and predatory eyes, a name that was his own instead of something given to him unsolicited, and people besides Zilch—still ever-present, ever-loyal, ever-loving—who cared about him. Who would care if he lived or died, and missed him when he wasn't here.

His whole life, he's been fighting to *become*: to find who he was supposed to be, and where, and what he was meant to fight for, not just struggle against.

Now, for the first time, he's starting to feel as if he *is*.

Rowan doesn't answer, but they don't pull away either, nor does Regan feel them stiffen, or hold their breath, or anything else that his hypervigilance would interpret as a negative. So he makes himself continue, hoping that each new word he stumbled upon would be the right one to tell this new, beautiful, terrifying truth.

"I know you now, the real you. Your kindness, your patience—your smart jokes that take me a second to get. How dedicated you are to making life actually livable here, and how... healing it is to be around you. It's good, it's... warm. And how strong you are. How strong you have to be, to stay that soft in a place like this." He licked his dry lips, and shut his eyes. "I don't just think I love you anymore. I know I do. But for the right reasons this time."

He knows it now. He knows it like he knows there was still a moon and stars beyond Parole's barrier-sky, the way he knows that even if the world outside knows nothing of their lives in Parole now, that someday they would, people would talk about them, and they would remember.

Silence. He keeps his eyes closed.

Until a warm hand touches the side of his face, stroking his cheek down to the bottom of his neck frill, then back up again. Regan sucks in a little gasp and leans into Rowan's palm, the way he's stopped questioning, the way he always does because it feels right every time. He feels Rowan roll over onto their side to face him, and when he opens his eyes it's right into theirs, familiar blue and soft.

"I meant what I said before," Rowan says, and they don't quite sound shocked or hesitant. Closer to awed. Regan doesn't know what that meant exactly, but it isn't an immediate yes, so, naturally, he fights the urge to disappear again right here.

"That it's just some weird savior feelings thing?" He sighs.

"No," Rowan says, and now he gets the impression they're picking their words very carefully. "I did say that then. But I also said that I wasn't going anywhere. And I'm still not." They pause, arm still around him, and Regan holds his breath as they hold him close. "I don't want to go anywhere you aren't."

"Do you mean...?" Regan almost whispers, afraid to ask, more afraid not to.

"I think so," Rowan says, sounding every bit as stunned. "I've never felt anything like this before. I don't know what it's supposed to feel like. I never had a reason to wonder. A life without romance is nothing to be sad about—I never thought mine would have it, and that would have been fine. But when you came into that life... It's like you said. Maybe I'm different than I thought too, in some ways."

"No, no we're not that much," Regan shakes his head, not sure if he wants to laugh or cry or both. "At least you're not. Which is good, because I don't want you to be anything but who you are. That's who I want with me. If you want to be."

"Sometimes I don't think you know how brave you are," Rowan says, and he feels their laugh vibrate through his own chest where they press together. "Surviving all this time, staying true to who you are—a brave, beautiful, sweet boy. And saying all that—so I didn't have to!"

Regan laughs at that now, and it isn't nervous, not brittle, nothing but relief and real, unaccustomed, overwhelming joy.

"But I'm saying it now," Rowan whispers, and pressed their lips against his forehead.

As he gasps again, near tears of the best possible kind, Rowan gently brings their foreheads together and Regan's stinging eyes automatically slip shut again. This is one of his favorite intimate positions, this simple touch that always means safety and warmth, that always means always.

"I love you, Regan. The past few years have been... strange ones. For everyone, I think. And I don't know what's going to happen to us tomorrow or in a year, but I know that whatever does, I want you here with me to see it."

Regan's visions swims as his chest aches, feeling like it's glowing at the same time. He tastes salt. Would that be what Rowan tasted if...

"Can I kiss you?" He blurts, but for once, doesn't feel immediately mortified. He stays visible, too, baby steps. And then one giant leap. "Um, on the lips?"

"Please do."

Rowan smiles, and that was the last thing Regan sees before they connect and everything is happiness and warmth and confirmation, rightness, releasing everything that had once scared and weighed him down, crushing him into silence. This is the feeling of finally coming home after a very long journey, and at last being allowed to rest. But even as he's lost in this sweet and brave new world, the one thing he doesn't lose is himself. It's taken him a long time to find the person he was meant to be—to realize he was exactly that person—and, like Rowan, he's never letting them go.

Always Be You

SEVEN YEARS BEFORE CHAMELEON MOON

Warm. Quiet. Dark. One of Regan's favorite times of the day: late, after Library closing hours, but not so late that it was time to slip through shadows or run through crumbling streets. One of his favorite places: the secret, secure, safe back room filled with books and jars and his soft beanbag-chair nest and pile of blankets.

And one of his favorite people. His fingers moved through Rowan's soft, curly hair, hand coming to rest on the back of their neck, using the slight pressure to kiss them more deeply. Their quiet sigh and way they seemed to further melt in his arms told him he was doing it right.

Getting better at this.

The two of them had already been here for some time. They usually were. They were never in a hurry to reach their limits and fall asleep, because that meant an end to their time together that night, time that could otherwise be spent in warm embraces and slow, lazy kisses. Or just quiet talking for hours. Or not talking. Regan loved lying here and listening to their breath, their heartbeat—in their chest, an odd sensation for him after years with someone whose heart stayed safe in a jar in this very room—just as much.

They weren't talking much tonight. Regan didn't get many opportunities in his life to feel this completely relaxed, so blissfully, almost dreamily happy, so he focused all his attention on enjoying every second. And on Rowan.

There was a lot to learn about one another. Probably more than most, considering Regan's first and only experience so far was with a much-beloved partner with a not-quite-living body. This was full of surprises. Like feeling a heartbeat. Watching someone actually breathe as they slept. And what it was like to feel this warm. Until now, no matter how heated things got, Regan had been the only one whose temperature rose at all. Now, for the first time in his life, Regan held someone warmer than he was, and never wanted to let them go. Sometimes he wondered if this was how Zilch felt, holding him. It was a good feeling.

There were a lot of good feelings. Some of it was the contrast. Regan was all thin, angular limbs covered in smooth, cool scales. Rowan was so warm he wanted to curl his entire body around theirs and soak in their heat like a lizard on a sun-kissed stone. But a rock was an unfair comparison, he thought, because except for their hooves and horns, they were also soft in all ways. Like their wonderful, fur-like wool Regan loved to run his hands through and sleep with his cheek nestled in, and their waist Regan wrapped his wiry arms around, their soft belly pressed against his own; his was much slimmer but his scales were softest there too.

Regan loved them so much he thought his heart might burst. It didn't, but it was certainly pounding as Rowan's hands—gentle, like everything else about them when they were with Regan—went to the loose frill of skin around his neck. As they stroked down its hanging folds he let out a soft, involuntary sound, half-sigh, half-moan. Just as automatically, his frill trembled in reply. He didn't need a mirror to know it would be a couple shades darker than usual. Some people blushed in their cheeks, Regan did in his frill.

And just like his frill, he felt his entire body start to tremble. His heart pounded under Rowan's hand, which he realized had moved down to press against his chest. Regan leaned into the touch, feeling the shared heat rising between them, sure he could feel Rowan's heart speed up as well as he closed his hand over one of their hips, other hand stroking their side.

More touch. He wanted more closeness, more warmth, more sweetness. More of this. More of *them*. Just more Rowan. What and how, he wasn't entirely sure. He just knew they were pressed as close together as they could be, no space between them, and they still weren't close enough.

When he broke the kiss it was to suck in a gasp. Rowan's hand was still on his chest, and the other had slipped beneath his frill, fingers brushing across the point of his racing pulse.

Then Rowan's soft voice was in his ear. Saying something. It took a moment for him to sort the syllables into something he recognized. "Regan..."

Any other time, any other way, he would love the sound of Rowan whispering his name. But now, it felt like a vaguely dissonant note in what had up to this point been his favorite song. Their voice was tinged with uncertainty. It sounded like the same confusion starting to creep into his own head like a very unwelcome guest.

"What is it?" Regan's voice came out more breathless than he expected. All of this was more than he expected. His head spun. It felt like they'd just been in a speeding car, and someone had slammed the breaks.

"Is this..." Rowan stopped, and slowly, that same uncertainty filled their face as well as their voice. Their bright blue eyes flicked down, and they seemed to realize where they were for the first time. They didn't move or recoil, but they did take in both of their hands, then their bodies, and when they looked back up at Regan, it was as if they were seeing him for the first time too. "What is this?"

"I don't..." Realization fell on Regan like a bucket of ice water. He didn't feel warm at all anymore. Instead he felt the beginnings of the telltale shiver right before he vanished from view. "Let's just—stop for now, take a break, okay?"

"Agreed," Rowan seemed to know they didn't have much time before everything went to hell in any number of possible ways, and talked fast. "But Regan, don't go, please, you don't have to—"

"I'm so sorry—" he broke off as he rapidly backed off. He coughed suddenly, taking himself by surprise and interrupting the vanishing shiver. Perfect. His body was betraying him with a stress-asthma attack along with the involuntary disappearing act at the worst possible moment.

"Don't be sorry, just take a deep breath." Rowan paused, still looking a bit disoriented. "I'm doing the same. Regan, stay with me, please."

He had a feeling they meant in more ways than one. So he fought down the urges to run, disappear, and cough, and focused on his breathing. And tried *not* to focus on why he was now somehow ashamed to look Rowan in the eye.

"Okay," he said after several seconds, when he could speak again without his voice catching in his throat and turning into a cough. "I'm okay now. Are you okay?"

"Yes," Rowan said, and Regan hoped he imagined any hesitation before they answered. "Do you want to talk about—"

"I'm s—I know you just said not to be sorry but I still am," Regan lurched upright, starting to wriggle out of the covers that just made him feel restricted. "I didn't mean to do that. I mean, I don't know what— that's not true. I do know. At least I think I do. Not for sure, but—"

"Regan." As before, Rowan's quiet voice brought him back to the present. They hadn't moved, and they were still looking at him, but in a different way than before. Less confused, more concerned, but still not what he was afraid he might see. No blame—and more importantly, no fear or pain. "I was... caught up in it too."

"Yeah, but you weren't..." he stopped. Ran back over the past few minutes in his head, then the past hour. Everything had happened slowly, then very fast. But surely he couldn't have missed something so glaring. He'd been wrapped up in the beautiful moments, wrapped up in Rowan entirely. How could he have been so mistaken? "Were you?"

"I was..." Rowan stopped too. Regan knew their face well enough to pinpoint the exact moment they started to do what he'd just done: start playing their evening back in their mind, looking for the moment their paths had diverged. "Enjoying being here with you."

"Right, me too," he agreed with some relief when they finally continued.

"Loved the snuggling, favorite part of my night. Kissing was very nice—you're getting better at that."

"Thank you, with the tongue, I—anyway, yes, same, me too." Regan almost laughed. So far, so good.

"And then we..." Rowan paused. Regan held his breath. "I think we got a little ahead of..."

"Yeah." Regan's eyes dropped. So did his stomach. "Me too."

"It's not that I wasn't enjoying it—"

"Rowan, please," Regan shook his head. If he was feeling anything now it was sick. "You don't have to do that. God, I never wanted to—"

"No, that's not what I'm saying," they said firmly. "I wouldn't lie about this. And I wouldn't accept anything that hurt me. Not for anyone. Not even you."

"Oh. Well, good." He hadn't thought anything could make him feel better now, but that did. "I just couldn't ever..."

"And you didn't. Let that go. You didn't hurt me, and you won't do it by accident." Rowan smiled, and the knot in his stomach loosened by a small degree. It always did when he saw that. "Believe me, I'll let you know long before that happens."

"Okay." Regan let out a breath, and a long with it a great deal of painful tension. "The world is just full of... bad things. Especially this place."

"I know," Rowan said quietly. "We've both seen a lot of bad. But good's still around too."

"Yeah, I know. You help me remember that." He didn't continue, but wasn't remotely satisfied either. But if the words he wanted existed he couldn't find them, so instead he stared into the middle distance, perfectly still aside from the nervous flicker in and out of his tongue.

"Regan. I *was* enjoying it—being with you, kissing you, you touching me. I love it more than anything—I love *you* more." Like it always did, Rowan's voice cut through the haze of anxiety and rang true. Like always, Regan believed them. "And that's why this is so... confusing."

"Oh my God, thank you for saying it." Regan slumped forward and buried his face in his hands. "Nothing makes sense. This isn't like how it is with Zilch. I mean, it kind of is, it almost is, but there's this—I don't know!"

"Do you think this is what sexual attraction feels like?"

Regan choked again, this time apparently on his own tongue. "What?"

"Sexual attraction," Rowan repeated, sounding remarkably casual, but thoughtful. "Do you think this is it?"

"I don't know?" Regan managed to say, also remarkably casually considering the fact that he was contemplating disappearing again, completely voluntarily this time. "Do you?"

"I've never felt it before, personally, so I have no idea."

"Well, neither have I!" He turned to look Rowan fully in the infuriating, adorable face. "At least, I don't think so! Wouldn't you know if you had?"

"I'm honestly starting to wonder..." Rowan's tone was hesitant, but not fearful or upset. Curious, yes, and almost shy, but still nothing Regan expected or feared. When he hesitated in turn, they gently took one of Regan's hands in theirs, and the last of his shame began to fade away. "Something was definitely happening. Clearly. It wasn't a bad thing—but it is getting a little mixed up in my head."

"Well, what did you feel?"

"I was definitely... engaged," Rowan reflected, but they still sounded uncertain. "My body was, anyway."

"Yeah you were." Regan had to smile.

The urge to touch Rowan again, reach out and stroke their face, lay a hand on their chest was strong. It wouldn't take much to feel their breath speed up, their heart begin to pound. Or try for the opposite. He knew if he shifted closer and put an arm around them, they'd instantly rest their head on his shoulder, and they'd both do the automatic-by-now re-arrangement of Regan's head around their horns. Then Rowan's whole body would relax, and their pulse would slow just from his presence. Regan's own heart ached. But then he remembered their voice when they'd said his name, seeming to wake him from a fever dream. The uncertainty in their eyes, something he never wanted to see there again.

"But that's not enough, is it?" he asked. "Your body was into it, but your head wasn't?"

"It was, but not in the same direction." They didn't sound unsure anymore. Relief flooded through Regan. Someone knew what they were doing here. "Touching, kissing, being close to you, that's what I love. It has nothing to do with sex—but my body and brain don't always agree. And no matter what my body does, if I don't go along with it..."

"It doesn't change a thing," Regan finished, just as certain. Why was it so much easier to be that certain about someone else rather than himself? "Doesn't mean yes. You say yes or no. You're still in charge, you're still you."

That seemed to comfort them greatly, because they visibly relaxed, tension dropping out of their shoulders and face. They'd been just as confused and alarmed as he was, Regan thought. That shouldn't happen. Especially not if he was a reason in any way. "How about you, what did you feel?"

"I was so happy," Regan said quietly, looking down at their joined hands. "I wanted to stay like that forever. Holding you, touching you. It just felt so good, having you in my arms, you're so..." his breath caught, and he wasn't sure if he was going to cough again, so he just took a long, deep inhale instead. Held it like holding Rowan's hand. Let it out slowly. By the time he was done, he could breathe.

"I'm with you so far," Rowan said, and when he looked over, they were smiling. "There's nowhere I'd rather be."

"I just wanted to be close to you. Feel all of you. So I guess I got..." He searched for a word that would describe the amazing feeling of floating, while at the same time being so aware of every inch of his skin pressed against Rowan's and still not close enough to them, every bit of him alive with the heat building between them and from within, like there was a sun in his chest and with every beat it burned brighter and hotter, moving with Rowan's hand down his chest to his solar plexus, to-

"Excited?"

"Yeah." That had to do. "That felt different than the whole time I've been with Zilch. I love them so much, but it's... it's just different. I've never felt that."

"Desire?"

"Yeah. For you, and what we were doing, but just... more of that. More of what I think we were moving toward."

"Sex." Like always, Rowan just said what he couldn't.

"I think so." He shut his eyes as if that could keep the sinking feeling from overtaking him again. It didn't really work. "I didn't expect it. I just never thought—I've never looked at someone and thought—hey, I want—I still don't think I would! I don't even look at strangers and think—anything!"

"Because you don't know them?"

"No! I've never understood how anyone does—even just kissing, or little things like that, how do you do that with someone you don't know? Or want to?"

"It does take a great deal of trust," Rowan said, sounding thoughtful again. "At least for me. And you, I strongly suspect."

"I still can't imagine it happening again," Regan shook his head. "And I don't really know why it did now with you, I—I'm sorry."

"Don't be sorry," Rowan said more vehemently than they had before. "You're still you."

"What?" His neck frill twitched again, this time out of rising panic. He'd heard the words but not quite understood them; they just added another layer of confusion.

"What you said a minute ago. You found something new about yourself tonight—but you're still you. Nothing changes that."

"Seems like the kind of thing that would," Regan muttered. But, like it always did when Rowan sounded that sure about anything, his panic subsided, leaving heaviness in its place.

"Life is made up of shades of gray, including sexuality spectrums. Or asexuality for that matter," Rowan said in the oddly conversational tone they sometimes slipped into when discussing things Regan had a hard time even naming out loud. "You can fall on any infinite number of points, or fluctuate between them. Looks like we're just a little farther apart than previously estimated, that's all. You might sometimes experience sexual attraction when you're with someone you love and trust. I don't think I will—but it doesn't mean I love or trust you any less. Just because our orientations are farther apart doesn't mean we have to be."

"You know how this works," Regan looked up, feeling caught between hopeful and even more overwhelmed. "Everything you just said, all of this. But you were confused just now too?"

"I'm confused a lot more than just now," Rowan laughed in a way that never made Regan feel like he was being laughed at. But now he actually felt like he got the joke. "I try to learn all I can, but it's never enough. You can spend your life trying to figure out who you are and what you want. And you can still be surprised. I never thought I'd be this close to anybody—emotionally or physically. That's part of what threw me for a loop."

"Well, good. I guess. At least it's not just me."

"I don't think anything ever is. Feelings are messy, they can overlap even if you have yourself pretty well established. Try not to worry. However you end up is fine." They gave his hand a squeeze. "Some things don't change."

"Okay," he said quietly. Somehow Rowan's easy explanation—or maybe acceptance—left him calmer than anything else so far. "So, if you never have... the attraction feelings, but I do sometimes, Then how do we... work this?"

"Same way we have up until this point, if that's all right with you."

"Yeah, definitely," Regan nodded, but still seemed a bit more anxious than his customary level. "Because you're not... I mean, you could never... could you?"

Rowan was quiet for a few seconds, but it felt like much longer. "If I could with anyone, it would be with you. You said you wanted more of what we were doing, heading toward sex. For me... there was no 'heading toward,' I just wanted to stay there with you, in all the sensations. I love skin on skin—or scales. The smell of you, even the taste. The senses. The sensual. Just experiencing every sensation and emotion fully, I love that. But sex is... not connected to any of that, not for me. It's something else entirely. Something I still don't want, or need."

"That's fine!" Regan almost laughed. The wave of relief was so strong it made him lightheaded, and his head spun in a different way than it had before. He couldn't really say why, or why now he couldn't stop smiling. Maybe just because they finally both had answers for sure. "I mean—is that fine? Are we okay?"

"Of course," Rowan smiled back. "Now there just won't be any confusion next time."

"Next time?" Regan's stomach felt fluttery instead of heavy and sinking.

"I certainly hope there is one. You were right, Regan," they said, stroking his face. He leaned into the touch and let his eyes drift shut again. "I learned something about myself tonight too. Or confirmed it.

Doubting, questioning, they're normal—and if you find something new in yourself, that's good. Or maybe you get through it and find that you always were who you thought, but now with more strength and confidence."

"What did you find?" he asked sleepily.

"That none of what happened tonight changes who I am. Or the way I feel about you. We might have more to learn about ourselves and each other, but I want you with me while we do."

"That's good," Regan murmured, letting himself be pulled back into his nest of blankets and pillows. He was suddenly exhausted after all this physical and emotional upheaval, and very glad to find himself in the right place for a nap. Close against Rowan's warm side, where he belonged. "I like it here."

"So do I. And I love you."

"Love you too," he said, certain of that if nothing else.

Stitches

ONE WEEK AFTER CHAMELEON MOON

Finn held the needle so tightly his fingertips were beginning to turn white and his entire hand shook. He stared at Zilch's arm, the torn skin and the stitches he hadn't made yet, and nothing else existed. His entire world shrunk to the head of a needle, on where it had to go. He heard nothing, saw nothing else. He'd thought that threading the thing would be the hard part, that surely, after that was done, the rest would be easy. He was wrong.

He heard something. A voice. A word? He couldn't tell. His tunnel-vision held steady even if his hand didn't.

Until something touched his wrist—the one he hadn't moved in almost a full paralyzed minute—and he jumped, gasping. The hand around his shaking wrist was firm, holding it steady even as the rest of him gave a wild, startled jerk.

"Breathe," Zilch whispered for a second time, and Finn only now identified the sound from before. "You stopped again."

"I can't do this." Finn shook his head, needle and thread falling from his now-numb fingertips to land with a soft clink on the counter beside them. "I'm sorry, Zilch, I just can't."

"Yes." Zilch's rasping voice was even drier after they'd been nearly burnt to a cinder. "You—"

"We need to find someone else," Finn insisted with increasing desperation where he wished for conviction. Actually, he wished he didn't have to say the words at all. He wished more than anything for the bravery to give Zilch what they needed. To say yes. "Like Danae, she could do this in a second. Or Evelyn."

"They could." Zilch did not let go of his wrist. "Don't want them to. Want you."

"Anyone *but* me would be better!" Finn protested. "I've never done anything like this! I can't even hold the needle! I'm not the one we want fixing anyone."

"Need you fixing me." Despite their charred face, Zilch's eyes were clear and stayed unhesitatingly on Finn's.

"No, you need someone who actually knows what they're doing." Finn let his arm drop, finally breaking their contact. "We need Rowan!

Or Regan! Or even—" he broke off, seeing the way Zilch's eyes fell, so expressive even now, the pain in them clear, sharp, and devastatingly deep. "I'm sorry," Finn whispered, clapping one hand over his mouth.

"Don't," they said, eyes closing, and Finn shut his eyes too, chest physically aching. He wasn't sure which of their hearts was in pain. Maybe both.

"Zilch, I'm so sorry."

"No. I meant, don't be sorry." They spoke again, more gently. Finn looked up to see that Zilch wasn't staring at the ground as he'd expected. Instead, they met his eyes with the same deep sadness, but without hesitation—or blame.

"I just meant that it'd be better if we had someone who'd done this before," Finn tried again, in a voice softer than most people ever heard, or knew he was capable of using. "Someone you trust."

Zilch remained quiet and still for a moment, holding his gaze with a look even he had trouble reading. Finally, their crooked mouth stretched and curled into one of the strange expressions most people found frightening, but Finn recognized as a smile. But this was an unusual one even for them. It didn't quite chase away the loss lingering in their mismatched eyes, and it flickered and died too soon, like a candle burning down to the end of its wick.

"I trust them," they said at last in a voice like a faint wind through a crack in a stone wall. "But I trust you too."

"You miss them." Finn spoke almost as softly, afraid of somehow breaking the fragile spell of connection and understanding he felt falling over both of them.

"Yes. I miss them both." Their words came out slowly, like Zilch was turning them around in their mouth like lifting up unfamiliar stones, finding what lay beneath both painful and cathartic. Gingerly, they flexed the hand Finn wasn't working on, relatively undamaged but still burned black. "I miss them like... missing an arm. But I will see them again."

"You sound really sure about that."

"I am."

"How can you be?" And which one of them was Zilch trying to reassure? Were they just telling Finn a secret, or admitting it to themself for the first time? Whatever it was, he felt somehow honored to witness this moment, whether a revelation or a discovery.

"Because I trust them with more than just myself." Zilch's smile was back, and now it was real. Finn had the feeling they weren't surprised at the question—or much he said or did by now. Being that familiar to someone was a nice feeling. Warm. "I trust that they will find one another. They will come home. We will be together again. The way I trust you."

They held up their injured arm again, and Finn raised the needle and thread. This time, his hands didn't shake.

"Okay," he said. "Let's try this one more time."

Memento Ignis

SEVEN YEARS BEFORE CHAMELEON MOON

Annie had never been down this far under the library. She knew the building—one of the most secure and biggest left standing in Parole—stretched down a few more floors. But she'd never completely mapped the dim halls and tight, creepy stairwells that twisted like a multi-level maze. It was a little scary down here, but the fun kind of scary that made her want to explore, like an adventurous spelunker. She'd been told a few times not to go down here alone, by most of the adults of her life at one point or another—but those were kid rules, and she was eleven, definitely not a kid anymore. Eleven was practically thirteen, which was

practically sixteen, which was practically an adult. It seemed so simple to her, even if nobody else seemed to understand this.

Besides, she was bored. Both of her parents were meeting with Garrett Cole, which she wasn't strictly supposed to know about, but since she did, was absolutely supposed to keep her mouth shut about. Because once they were done discussing whatever it was that needed doing in Parole, both her parents would go back to a SkEye logistics center where they pretended to be good and obedient employees. Parole might be the only city in the world with actual superheroes, but her parents' jobs were just as dangerous, and they didn't even have powers. The thought of them basically spying on Eye in the Sky, which spied on everyone, fighting from the inside and telling Garrett its secrets was exciting. It made her proud. It also made her feel sick to think about for too long, because even eleven-year-olds knew what happened to Parole people who got caught being heroes.

There was a difference between good exciting and bad, and there were too many scary things in Parole anyway. She'd rather be bored. But being bored alone still sucked.

Rowan could be fun to talk to (depending on the subject, provided they didn't get on one of their nerdier tangents), but they were pulling another all-day clinic shift upstairs. It wasn't good to bother them when they were trying to help people, and they'd be too tired to do anything but crash once they came off it.

Regan had disappeared somewhere, maybe off on a Runtime mission, or maybe just disappeared into thin air, the way that he did.

Zilch too, so they were probably together. When the two of them had come to stay here a year ago, she'd found Regan fascinating to look at, with his pretty green scales like a dragon out of a fairy tale. Spots of him were kind of iridescent almost, when they were clean. But staring made him nervous, and eye contact too, which she understood all too well, and that just made her like him more.

Zilch had taken longer to get used to. She'd never been afraid of them, exactly, but they were one of the weirder Parole people she'd seen, towering over her head and made of all kinds of different colors of skin and sizes of body parts—all of which Rowan sewed together like a big quilt or puzzle. Zilch didn't talk much, which was actually fine, since Annie preferred hanging out and reading (about engines or cars, usually) or drawing (also cars, most of the time, but lately she couldn't stop thinking about motorcycles) in silence, and just having a friend there who wouldn't bug her with a lot of chatter that made her nervous was nice. Zilch seemed to think it was nice too, because she'd look up to see their usual stare softening into something that looked calm and content. It made her happy.

She'd had good friends her own age once, who she would've happily gone to find, but they weren't here anymore. She hadn't seen Indra or Shiloh since the barrier went up. They'd gotten out. Annie hadn't. She guessed she should be happy for them, but sometimes it was hard to feel anything but jealous and depressed, or sometimes mad at them for escaping and leaving her here. It wasn't like they'd meant to, like any of them had gotten a choice, or asked for any of this, but it still wasn't fair.

And Gabriel was gone without a trace, disappeared the same day the other two did. The way a lot of people had, that day. Maybe he'd gotten out too. She hoped he did. Then she could be jealous and mad at him too, instead of just sad.

Mostly Annie tried not to think about them at all, but it wasn't easy.

Parole did have a few kids around, probably even some in or near the library right now, but Annie didn't always get along with them. She didn't understand them, what made them laugh or cry, and she usually ended up saying something wrong, or them saying something that made her feel stupid. They definitely didn't understand her. Sometimes she forgot how words worked, or just how English words worked, and everybody thought that was really weird—and then of course she couldn't explain that it was just a thing that happened, and she'd remember how to talk like she usually did again soon. It all made her feel like an alien stuck on the wrong planet, or a real Parole Freak even though she was a normal, Chrysedrine-free human. As far as she knew.

She hadn't even seen Ash all day, which annoyed her the most. You couldn't pick most of your family, but if she could pick godfathers, she'd pick him every time. He always understood her, or at least tried to, which was better than most people, outside of her parents and the few Parole folks she was starting to think of as family too.

That left her alone today. And she wasn't bored enough to go outside alone—that was the bad kind of exciting, the scary type. So she came down here to explore the library's murky depths instead. Forget what over-worried adults thought; this was inside, how dangerous could it be inside? Besides, there was someone else down here now. She wasn't *alone*. Annie could hear footsteps against metal up ahead, light coming out of a cracked door that had never been open before. Eagerly, she hurried up to the door and pushed it the rest of the way open.

Then froze in the doorway.

She hadn't known the library stretched all the way down to the fire.

In the center of the room was a depressed metal grate, a hood vent stretching down from the ceiling, and in the middle of the depression burned a roaring fire. Annie had seen buildings burn before. Parole had always been a powder keg, and last year, someone had struck a match. Soon, the fires were everywhere, eating up entire blocks at a time. She hadn't been caught in a blaze herself, but she was painfully aware of how everybody talked about it, like falling into it was inevitable. She had nightmares about fire, just like everybody else who lived here, probably. And to see it right here, inside, was something out of a nightmare in itself.

She barely registered that there was something *in* the fire, something oblong and wrapped in a white sheet. She was focused on the flames, and then, on the figure before them.

Ash stood in front of the fire pit, looking lost in thought as he watched the flames lick around the shrouded shape. But he didn't look worried at the fire indoors, seeming pensive and totally calm—until he caught sight of her standing in the doorway and gave a little startled jump that was almost comical for someone of his substantial height.

"Annie! Hi," he said, clearly nervous and somehow guilty, almost like he'd been caught doing something he wasn't supposed to. Or at least something she wasn't supposed to see. "What, uh, what are you doing down here?"

She couldn't answer. All she could do was stare at the fire in the middle of the room, so bright it seemed to eat up everything, all the shadows and all the air and maybe even her.

"We're in the fire?" she asked in a small voice, fighting panic. If Ash wasn't afraid, she wasn't afraid, she told herself. But it was hard to keep calm with Parole's worst nightmare, as well as one of hers, in the room with them.

"No—no, we're not that far down," he said, crossing the room in just a couple long-legged strides to stand between the fire and Annie, letting her focus on something that didn't scare her. "This is just a room where we burn stuff and then let it out into the fire. See, the ceiling vent collects the smoke so it doesn't get the room all smoky, and the grates down there on the floor let the ashes and everything fall down a long chute, and *that* goes into the fire. It's all part of the same thing, so this is just kind of giving it back."

Annie took a step closer, peering curiously at the white-wrapped object. All at once, she knew what it was. Not just a sheet, a shroud, wreathed in flames. She'd seen that combination before, in a fuzzy, far-off memory from when she really had been a kid. People crying. Her mom holding her hand while she shifted uncomfortably, unsure exactly what was going on, but not liking the heaviness in the air.

"There's a person in there, isn't there?" she asked, mad at herself when it still came out shaky.

"Uh..." Ash cast a look over his shoulder, like he had to check, to see if it was still there. When he looked back at her, though, the uncertainty and surprise was gone from his face, and he looked her steadily in the eyes. "Yeah. Yes, there is. I'm laying her body to rest."

"I'm sorry," she said, a sinking feeling in her stomach. "I shouldn't be here."

"No, you..." He stopped, maybe seeing the way her face fell. His own softened. "You didn't do anything wrong. I left the door open. And it's not—not really a bad thing you walked in on, just..." he shook his head, a lopsided smile crossing his face. "Aw, it's not like it's a secret. Just another part of life in Parole. Come on in."

"Who was that?" she asked as she stepped forward, eyes still on the shrouded body in the middle of the room, lower than her feet. Sort of the opposite of what she'd seen before, then, like a reverse pyre.

"Well, I didn't actually know her," Ash said, still sounding a little awkward, but less so than before. "But I know she did a lot of good for this city. We owe her a lot. Her name was Sarah."

"Why are you doing this?" she asked, turning her curious gaze onto him instead of the fire. He was easier to look at, but this was all still confusing. Fortunately, Ash was one of the people in her life who explained hard concepts and made them easy to understand, if not to accept.

"Because, everybody in Parole has a job, or uh, something they're good at, to help it keep going," Ash said, and she didn't need to understand most people very well to know he was still caught off-guard. Not quite making it up as he went, but close enough to it. "This is mine. Part of it, anyway. Has been since... about a year after the bubble went up, I guess."

"I've heard people talk about you. They have a name for you. *Reaper*," she said in a low voice that made it feel like a secret. People always talked about it in the same quiet voices, exchanges that, like the more dangerous things her parents did, she definitely wasn't supposed to overhear, but managed to anyway. It had taken her a long time to piece together that when they said that, *Reaper*, in that low, secretive tone, they meant Ash. Once she did, there was no getting it out of her head. "That is you, right?"

"Yeah..." Ash grimaced, fiddling with the chain around his neck and the shark's tooth at the end, and giving her a wary look, like he was actually afraid of what *she* might say. "Kind of a scary name, but someone has to do it."

"I like it," she said with a slow smile. It was true. The name sounded cool and tough and not afraid of anything. Definitely the good kind of exciting. "Why?"

"Why what?" he asked, looking a little puzzled. Sometimes adults didn't follow Annie's train of thought, even if it seemed completely logical to her.

"Why does someone have to do this job? Burning dead people?"

"That's not my whole job. But, uh, sometimes... people get into very tough situations," Ash said, haltingly, like he was trying to find the words. She knew how that felt. Words could be very hard to come by sometimes. Maybe for other people too. Annie wasn't very patient when it came to most things, but this she understood. This, she could wait for. "And when it looks like they're not going to make it out of it, that's when they call me in. I'm really good at getting into hard-to-reach places, picking people up, and getting them out again."

"Bet you've saved a lot of people." Annie could imagine this very well. Ash didn't have superpowers either, but he'd never needed any to be strong and brave and someone who helped people smaller than he was. He never needed them to make her feel safe.

"Yeah, I like to think so," Ash said, and smiled, a much slower and less confident one than his usual grin. There were a lot of different kinds of smiles, and she'd never seen this one before, not with him. It looked... relieved. "I like it when I get to do that. Definitely my favorite part of the job. Heh, don't fear the reaper, sweet child o'mine."

He actually laughed, and Annie chalked it up to one of the many adult jokes she didn't get. Another day, she might have asked what was so funny. Right now, however, her mind was elsewhere.

"But... she..." Annie's eyes traveled back to the burning body. The flames had completely overtaken it now, and she could hardly see the white cloth anymore.

"Sometimes I can't save people, no," Ash said, smile fading.

Her parents were terrible liars, and Ash wasn't much better. But he was almost always honest with her, like she knew he was being right now. If he wasn't telling the truth, he'd have no reason to look so sad.

"And that's the other part of my job," he continued. "Making sure people don't hurt anymore." She didn't know why he looked so sad about that. That was a good thing, wasn't it? "And getting them home for the last time so their loved ones can say goodbye. And making sure they're safe. Making sure no one will mess with their bodies. When I get called in, whoever needs me knows that I'll fight like heck to get them out safe... but if I can't, I'll still bring them home."

Annie frowned, puzzlement taking the place of any lingering distress. "Who'd mess with a body? That's bad. That's really bad."

"Sure is." Ash gave her a long, considering look, then seemed to come to a conclusion, because he gave a little nod, probably to himself. "You know how a lot of our favorite people have cool superpowers?"

"Yeah." She smiled a little. It was always a good thought.

"Well, SkEye would love to know exactly how they work," Ash continued, sounding perfectly reasonable and calm, but his eyebrows came together, a crease showing between them. That was a signal to her, an almost-lying sign. He was telling the truth with his words, but not with his face. They didn't match. He didn't feel calm about this at all. "Because sometimes, they make people use their powers for bad things."

"Regan said something about that," Annie recalled. It had taken Regan a while too, but he was slowly starting to talk to her more than he did other people. He never talked to her like... well, like she was a kid. It felt like they were on the same level—mostly because he seemed actually comfortable around her, not afraid like he seemed most of the time. Maybe she didn't scare him because she was younger, or shorter, or a girl. He didn't seem to like big guys, or loud ones. Sometimes he'd just disappear. There were a lot of reasons to be afraid of people, and Regan seemed like he had a lot of them. "He said he and Zilch used to live at SkEye and they didn't like it."

"No, they didn't. They'd rather die than go back there." Ash paused, seeming to war within himself with something. As she carefully watched his face, Annie could see him make another decision, lick his lips, give another little nod, and push ahead. "Because even after they're dead... SkEye won't stop. They want to study our bodies and figure out new ways to hurt us. But they're not going to, because I won't let that happen. That's my real job—like your mom and dad. We make sure SkEye doesn't find out new ways to use us against one another."

Annie gave him a serious nod to let him know she believed him. But she didn't speak. She spoke when she could think of an actually important thing to say, and she couldn't right now. What could anyone say to something so frightening, and yet completely unsurprising? In the three years she'd lived inside a barrier bubble while the rest of the world went on without them, she'd stopped being surprised at how bad people could be. How much pain they could inflict without thinking, or because they thought it would be good for themselves. Maybe even because they really thought it was the right thing to do, and somehow that was scariest of all. But mostly, she thought about the body in the fire.

"What would you do if I died?" she asked after several seconds of silence.

Ash's bright blue eyes widened. He opened his mouth, then shut it again, and now he looked just like he did when he'd first seen her, like all of this was something she wasn't supposed to see. But he regained control just as fast, anxiety fading from his face in favor of determined calm. He was quiet for a few seconds, but then spoke with his regular confidence. "You're not going to die, so don't worry about that."

Annie frowned and crossed her arms, young face twisting into a scowl. "People die. You don't have to pretend they don't."

"I'm... not doing that," he sighed, broad shoulders dropping a little, like he was suddenly tired. "I'm just saying that you don't have to worry about it."

"Everybody dies," Annie said, unsatisfied and pouting. Maybe not the most mature thing in the world, but right now, the most satisfying. "I already know everything. I've been to funerals and stuff, before the bubble went up."

"I know—and I know death is... different here in Parole, than most other places." Ash took a deep breath and let it out, and that seemed to help. "It's everywhere, and you learn that fast—too fast sometimes, I think. It's a little late to keep that from you, and I wouldn't try either. I'm just saying that *you personally*, Anh Minh Le, do not have to worry about it any time soon."

She felt a little better—that part rang true, even if his first answer hadn't—but kept her arms folded. He still wasn't talking to her like he would someone else, someone older. She wouldn't be satisfied until he did. "You still don't have to protect me."

"Of course I have to protect you," he said, giving her a sideways look. Now he definitely wasn't talking to her like he would someone older. But he also wasn't talking to her like he would anyone else. He only used this tone with her, fond and amused, but not laughing at her. It seemed like he was laughing at himself sometimes, and that made her feel comfortable, but never made fun of. He might be laughing at himself, but he was *talking* to her. "I'd be a pretty cra—cruddy godfather if I didn't."

"You don't have to do that either. I already know a lot of swear words." Now she cracked a smile.

Ash's fuzzy blonde eyebrows came together again. "What kind of swear words?"

"Lots. Probably ones you don't even know."

He chuckled. "I'm not sure about that, kiddo."

"How many do you know in Vietnamese?"

"Okay, you got me there. Especially going by how... creative your mom can be in English when she's bugged." Ash rolled his eyes and raised his hands in a gesture of surrender. "Fine, I'd be *crappy* if I didn't try to protect you. The crappiest godfather in the world. And your mom and dad would never forgive me. Heck, *I'd* never forgive me. So no, you don't have to worry about dying or any of that, because it's not happening."

"...Okay," Annie said with a little nod of her own, after thoroughly examining that statement in her head. She accepted it, because she always did when Ash used that tone, still meant for her, but not laughing anymore, instead completely certain and sure.

Her dad, Duy Khoa, had a similar expression and tone of voice that came through when he got thinking about a goal or promise, something he was committed to entirely. She'd heard it another time she was where she wasn't supposed to be, hearing things she shouldn't. Like her mom, Tam Minh, crying, saying that they really were stuck here in Parole, they were trapped, Anh Minh was trapped in this death zone, she'd never have a normal life, and that's all she'd wanted for her daughter, a safe, healthy life free from fear. Her dad had gotten quieter as she got louder, and Annie had to strain to hear him say that they were here too, they would survive this as a family, and even if it wasn't the life they wanted, for themselves or her, that didn't mean it couldn't be a good life. An important life. He wasn't giving up. Annie decided that day, eight years old, that neither was she.

"Can I stay and watch?" she asked at last. Not giving up meant not running away. Not when somebody needed you. And right now, even if he was smiling on the outside, she'd seen past Ash's front, caught his microexpressions of sadness and some embarrassment, and worry. Worry about what she'd think? Worry about her? She didn't know exactly. But she did know that even if he'd never admit it or ask it of her or say it was her job to make him feel better, Ash needed her right now.

Ash smiled, his real, warm, relieved smile, and it made her feel warm inside. It made her feel like she'd read him right, like she'd made the right choice. It made her feel brave. A little like a hero. "You can do more than that. Feel like helping me out?"

Annie looked at the shrouded body in the flames, now partly losing its shape. It had been a person once, but wasn't anymore, in a lot of ways. "What do we do now?"

"We remember her."

Ash put his hands behind his back and dropped his head. Feeling it was the right thing to do, Annie did the same, closing her eyes and listening to his voice, feeling it in her chest and the soles of her feet. She felt everybody's voice in a different place, and that was where his lived, every time, but especially when it dropped like this. When he was talking about something that really mattered.

"We live or we burn, Sarah. We all have very different lives in here, but wherever we go, we know that much is true. If you have gods, find them. If you don't, and it's just your life here that mattered to you, know it mattered to us too, Sarah. It still matters, Sarah. You were a part of this strange, beautiful world, and it was better because you were in it, Sarah. And now we let you go, but every day we're still here, we'll know it's because of you, Sarah."

Annie cracked open one eye and peek up at Ash, when he paused for a bit. "Why do you keep saying her name?"

He didn't open his eyes or move. "Because if I'm the one doing this for someone instead of their family or friends, it means they don't have anyone else to remember them. So that's part of my job too—to remember them. I'm going to say their names and remember any time we met, even just for a minute. Remember the person they were, and what they did for us."

"What if you never met them?" she asked.

"I've met almost every Runtime operative." He opened his eyes now, and looked at her with a faint, subtle smile. "We're not that tight-knit, not like a team or club or anything, it's safer that way. But we do tend to get each other. You're right, sometimes I don't know them, like I didn't know Sarah. So then I think about the people I do know, and how I'd remember them. And how I'd want them to remember me. Almost everybody here is somebody's kid or parent or sibling, cousin or partner or friend. And even if they aren't, even if there's nobody to miss them..." He looked up at the metal ceiling, as if he was looking beyond it, at Parole's barrier-dome sky. "We were in here together. We understand things nobody else who hasn't lived in Parole would. So we share that, even if the whole world doesn't. Nobody's really alone."

Annie stayed quiet for a while, young face serious, orange in the firelight that still danced on every surface in the room. It showed no signs of dying down. It probably wouldn't for a long time, just like the fire far below. "You did good, Sarah. Thanks for being here."

They stood together quietly, and Ash put his four-fingered left hand on Annie's shoulder. They stayed like that for a long time, or for what seemed like a long time to Annie. She admittedly wasn't the best judge, especially in serious moments like this.

"Now what?" she asked when she didn't like the silence anymore. She was getting hungry anyway, and getting hungry made her antsy, but she still wanted to see this through to the end.

"Now, we figure out what we need to do to stay alive," Ash said, somber tone dropping away in favor of his usual cheerful voice. He didn't seem nearly as tired anymore, or worried. Or like he was faking it. "Because life goes on, and nobody who's died would want us to stop living."

"To stay alive?" Annie asked, confused again. Then her stomach growled, breaking the respectful quiet and betraying her failing attempts at mature composure.

"I think I know the first step," Ash grinned brightly and gently bounced his fist on her shoulder. "Who's hungry?"

"Me, I am!" Annie turned toward the door with renewed enthusiasm and some relief. Even if this was a very important room, she'd be fine if she never saw the inside of it again. It was hard enough when the person they were letting go and remembering was a stranger. She didn't want to be able to actually remember anyone here. "Hey, what's my job?"

"Huh?" Ash moved to catch up with her, but didn't seem to quite follow her logic. Again.

"You said everybody has a job in Parole. What's my job?"

"Your job is to grow up," Ash said easily, like the heaviness of the past several minutes hadn't happened, like he wasn't carrying it around with him, like it was just another day. Annie couldn't tell he was telling the truth or not, but this time she could let it go. "Your job is to figure out what you like, and what you don't like, and who you want to be. And then *be that* as hard as you can. And it's our job—your parents, mine, Rowan, all of us—to make sure you get to do that, and be happy."

Together, they left the room, the fire, and Sarah behind. Ash closed the door securely as they left, with a final look back, and one last small, to-himself nod. Behind the door, the fire still burned. Below them, it burned as well. Someday maybe it wouldn't burn at all. Annie hoped it wouldn't, but she was old enough to know that until a whole lot about her world changed, fire would be their day and night.

It was what they remembered, as they remembered each other.

You're Not Going That Way

Nobody had seen the sun, moon, or stars in Parole for ten years. Still, they had to be there. Even with a lethal barrier overhead and permanent smoke blocking out the sky. No matter how the ground trembled or the fire roared. Even if nobody in Parole could see them, the stars were still there. The same was true for the people they loved on the other side of the barrier, safe and living normal lives. For ten years, everyone in Parole survived on the hope that the outside world was clean, free of fire and soldiers and all the other horrors haunting their dreams and waking life.

Some things were eternal, they said. The world didn't change that easily.

They were wrong.

Anh Minh Le was used to riding a motorcycle through Parole's crumbling streets, and leaping craters of red-hot flame. Parole's jagged alleyways were narrow, choked with dangerous twists and turns as well as smoke. Now she sped down an empty highway cutting through miles of open desert, churning up a dust cloud in her wake.

In every direction, a dead, poison-ravaged landscape stretched as far as she could see. Her tinted helmet visor cut the glare from the white-bleached earth and harsh sun blazing down on a surreal, almost alien-looking landscape. When she'd first seen the outskirts of the Tartarus Zone, it had been like setting foot onto another planet and directly into a strange, new nightmare.

"We made it!" Her heart was slamming so hard and fast it felt like part of her bike's engine, like their acceleration ran on adrenaline, and she was just a heartbeat away from actually taking flight. "We actually did it!"

"Yeah we did!" Ash sat behind her. A lot more precariously than she'd like, since he was balancing a liquid-filled, reinforced jar between himself and her own, much smaller, body. In the jar floated a disembodied organ—a pancreas, if they were right. Neither of them were entirely sure, even if this particular probably-pancreas was very important to both of them. "Now let's keep making it. We still got shields?"

"We're good!" A faint energetic sphere shimmered around their speeding vehicle. They were surrounded by a tiny version of the barrier that surrounded Parole, but for a much different, less sinister reason. A shield, not a cage.

"Good! Then gun that thing, Annie, let her rip!"

Annie obliged and they picked up more breakneck speed. When Parole had collapsed and a lucky few—far too few—managed to escape, they'd stepped into a new world, one much wider, open and seemingly free, but just as treacherous. But just like in Parole, if they stayed alert, together, and very lucky, they might still survive.

One thing hadn't changed. Like always, they were running away from something, not toward it. There were Eyes out here too—they just weren't in the Sky anymore.

"They still after us?" she had to ask, before risking a look herself. She didn't have to turn around; her helmet projected a holographic rearview display, complete with warning lights. A huge, angular, mechanical shape loomed behind them, maybe a mile away, but distance didn't mean much out here. Just as surreal as everything else out here, it was a battleship with no ocean in sight—but far from grounded. Deadly if it continued pursuit. But it soon fell behind a rolling hill, lost from sight. She waited for it to resurface, but it didn't pursue. "Guess not."

"Don't count Sharpe out yet," Ash cautioned, giving her shoulder a pat that felt like half affection, half warning. Then he went right back to hanging onto the large jar with both hands again, wrapping his muscular frame around it like a protective cocoon. "He'll circle around for a while, but he always comes back. Doesn't know when to quit."

"Got it." She gripped the handlebars so hard it hurt.

They'd escaped from a collapsing city, traveled nearly three thousand miles, survived a poison wasteland she just learned existed, and recovered a stolen treasure right out from under SkEye's nose. They'd saved Zilch's life today, or gotten a good start. Hopefully they'd be able to save their own.

"Hey, don't worry, Spark Plug." Ash's voice softened; clearly he'd heard the tightness in hers. "You did great, we got a win today. And we don't know when to quit either."

"Sure don't." Annie managed to smile, though her stomach still churned as if they were out on a stormy sea instead of solid ground. Her head spun from the new, empty space, dizzying after spending ten of her eighteen years in a claustrophobic prison-city. Above them stretched the vast, too-bright blue, seemingly-infinite sky, and she made herself focus directly ahead. *Don't look up.* Being suddenly set free could be just as terrifying as being confined.

"We're gonna make it," Ash reassured her. "Just don't slow down, and don't look back."

"How far out are we?"

"From Parole?" Ash called from the far side of their small camp, from where he was busily fiddling with a small object on the ground. "Or from Meridian?"

"Anywhere. Everywhere." Annie shook her head, turning in a slow circle. She'd never really known what 'the middle of nowhere' meant until now. Or how beautiful it could be, even in the midst of devastation. Clean air—relatively, anyway. No choking smoke. They didn't have to wear masks here. "How far are we from the actual Tartarus Zone?"

"Not really sure," Ash answered, but she was only half-listening. "The place likes to move its edges around so much, it's hard to say. We're safe enough for the night, I feel good saying that."

The sun was setting over the widest, most open space she could ever remember seeing. Endless highway in both directions, stretching away until it disappeared. Endless sky, graduating from red-orange to deep purple. More road than she could ever run or fly or speed down on any pair of wheels.

She stopped turning, and caught sight of Ash's face as he stood up, dwarfing her as he always did, and something about this made her clamoring anxiety quiet. Having to look up into his face felt familiar, but even he seemed small out here in the endless expanse. Red-orange afterimages of the unaccustomedly bright sun still danced in front of her eyes, but she thought she caught a glimpse of deep sadness in his before it was gone. "What?"

He shrugged lightly, tossing a nod up to the darkening sky. "I know, right? Ten years in a fishbowl will do that to you. Except I was actually old enough to remember what a sunset looked like."

"Yeah, um..." She shook her head, trying to clear some of the dizzy wonder from the sky's brilliant yellows and magentas. "I kind of forgot colors like that even existed. Except, you know. In fire."

His smile faded and he ran a hand through his dirty-blonde hair. Whatever sorrow she thought she'd seen didn't resurface, but he did look exhausted. "Yeah. Hopefully we'll run into less of that out here. Two thousand miles away from Parole should be far enough."

"Tartarus doesn't have fire, does it?" The question was out before she decided to ask. Thinking too hard about what lay ahead still made her freeze. It was like looking up at the endless sky. Too big. If Annie hadn't compulsively plucked out her eyebrows and the hair on both sides of her head years ago, from overwhelming feelings of dread exactly like this, she would have reached up and started picking again right then. It definitely wasn't a fashion statement, but the no-eyebrows, punk-fauxhawk look did go oddly well with her studded leather jacket and giant motorcycle. She'd take whatever mixed blessings she could get.

"Nah. Just gotta be careful of the air, turn on the filters if we run into a storm—and that's if we go further in." Ash gave his head a decisive shake. "Which is not on the agenda. Meridian's only five hundred miles away, and it's a straight shot from here. We'll be there before you know it. And don't worry about Sharpe bringing SkEye down on us," he placed another object on the ground—a metallic disc the size of a silver dollar—about three feet away from the last one, completing a large circle around the camp. "These awesome little thingies would go nuts if his ship came within a mile. But he won't. No matter how mad he is that we swiped that jar back."

"How do you figure that?" Ash rarely sugarcoated harsh realities when she asked him a direct question. So when he said they'd survive, she believed him.

"Oh, he's still out here somewhere. But he won't be looking for us, not tonight. He's dangerous but lazy. Make him work for us and we'll give him the slip every time." He gave her a nod. "Okay, arms and legs inside, ready to light 'em up."

As she watched, he flicked the final small disc. But instead of flipping up into the air, it projected a bright beam of light straight up. Then the beam split into two curving lines in opposite directions, running through the other coin-like censors. The lines connected to form a protective glowing circle around them.

"There. Better?"

"Yeah, long as it stays lit." Annie eyed the glowing circle a little warily. Once the boundary was complete, she breathed easier. But she wasn't ready to relax entirely. "I'm not worried about Sharpe or even Turret. It's..."

"You're not worried about human nasties, are you?" Ash asked in an oddly casual tone. "Well, this far on the outskirts, we're just not that likely to run into anything serious. Try to forget about it."

"Forget Tartarus?" She stared at him. "It's an evil wasteland across five states. It ate a hole in the ozone. And it's full of poison tornadoes, and monsters, and—"

"And we're not going through it, so *you don't have to worry about it.*" Ash fixed her with a level stare, emphasizing every word. "We're circling around the edge. I'd never take you through that place, not if we had any other choice. Right now we got choices."

"What about when we pick up Dr. Cole in Meridian? What if she wants to go through it or something?"

"Pretty sure she's spent ten years studying exactly why that's a bad idea. She'll want to get straight to Parole and get to work." He sounded sure enough for Annie to take him at face value and avoid panic a while longer. Then his eyes hardened. "She also has a hell of an incentive. Garrett left behind a lot of scared, grieving people behind, and avenging your husband is one powerful motivator."

"You sure she'll be able to help us, though?"

"Dr. Maureen Cole is the only one who's ever gone up against the Tartarus Zone and learned a goddamn thing besides 'it's big' and 'it's terrifying'—so when she says she knows how to help Parole, I believe her."

Annie gave a tentative nod and turned away, both from him and the darkness outside the protective circle. There were new monsters in the back of her head where Parole's fire had once been, and if she paid them too much attention, she'd never get to sleep. So she focused on something she could see and touch, something good and comforting.

After their frantic escape earlier that day, she'd secured the large, reinforced jar in one of her motorcycle's storage compartments. Now she dug it back out, setting it down in the middle of their camp. She sat down beside it, slowly turning it around as she checked and re-checked the thick surface for cracks.

"Still safe and sound?" Ash crouched down beside her, moving and speaking quietly as if not wanting to break whatever spell she'd begun to cast. It did almost look like she were gazing into a particularly strange crystal ball.

"Halfway safe," she answered, sounding faraway. "Still missing a heart. Kind of important."

"Zilch will be fine," Ash said, and for once she didn't look up to verify the conviction in his voice, still staring into the jar's depths. "That heart's out here somewhere, we'll find it."

Annie pressed her hands flat against its smooth surface. "Still. Can't believe that bastard didn't have it. I was so sure he had them both."

"You're surprised Sharpe didn't have a heart? I'm sorry," he said quickly as she looked up, eyes narrowed and eyebrows coming together, too-deep lines forming on her too-young face. "That was awful, really not the time—"

"It's not like I *want* SkEye to have Zilch's heart!" She ignored him, gripping the jar until her fingertips started to hurt. "No! No, I don't—"

"Annie. Breathe."

She sucked in a breath, held it. Let it out as slowly as possible. When she was done, she realized her fingers were shaking and turning white. "I just want to know why Sharpe only had *one* jar. What did he do with their heart? Didn't he take both?"

"Rowan and I saw him grab that one from the library in the collapse." Ash nodded at the pancreas jar. "And we, uh… stopped him from getting any more before he bugged out. He won't try that again. Sharpe knows if he messes with us he gets the horns. Ha, in Rowan's case, that's totally literal." He smiled but didn't meet her eyes, and she knew pressing for details about the confrontation would go nowhere. Not with Ash, or with his sibling Rowan, who until recently had run the secret shelter and clinic under the library. Also until recently, the place had been one of Parole's last, freest, safest havens. Whatever happened the day she'd escaped Parole as it collapsed and the library burned, neither one wanted to share it with her. "We saved every jar we could, but the heart wasn't there. So we have to assume Sharpe still has it. But he won't for long. We'll find Zilch's heart. We'll bring them all home safe, every missing piece."

Letting out a slow breath, Annie went back to staring at the gently floating piece of flesh. A bizarre thing to find comforting, but many strange things meant home and family in Parole. She could almost pretend she was back in a safe, secret room in the library. A room with many other jars. She could almost hear the gentle sound of hooves on carpet, imagine scales in soft light.

"Really... what do you think Sharpe wants with Zilch's organs?" she asked softly. "You don't think SkEye's trying to bring them back in, do you? Zilch would never do it. They'd never work for—"

"No. None of that. That's not how Sharpe thinks." Ash shook his head as he sat down opposite her. Something glinted against his chest, the familiar curved edge of a shark's tooth on a chain around his neck. It wasn't the kind of thing you saw often in Parole. Or out in the stretches of bone-dry land that made up the waste. She knew the bright shape just as well as the gently bobbing one in the jar. "I'm telling you the truth, I don't know."

"Take a guess." Annie's glare was almost a challenge, daring him to terrify her. Hit her with his best shot, the most brutal reality this new world had to offer. Tell her exactly how much danger threatened the people she loved.

He gave her a long, appraising look, then relented with a sigh. "My guess is that Major Turret's giving the orders, not him. Lieutenant Sharpe doesn't have the head for master plans. He's just the Major's instrument of destruction."

"That... doesn't make me feel better." Annie sighed, shoulders sagging, but not so much she crumpled in on herself, not so much she collapsed. "If Turret's in charge out here too, then Zilch—no, everyone could really be in trouble."

"Yeah." Ash nodded simply, didn't try to dispute it or comfort with pointless words. He held up his left hand, then curled the fingers except for the third—which was missing the last two joints. "Would've flipped Sharpe the bird as we jetted out of there, but wouldn't you know, he stole that years ago too."

Annie had to laugh. "And it would've probably tipped him off. A little."

"Ahh, he knows it's me anyway. Whenever somebody messes with him, he blames me, just how it goes by now. I do the same for him. I stub my toe, it's his fault. We've got a good thing going now." Ash cast a long, baleful look at the jar and the organ floating inside. "Except when other people get caught up in it."

"He's out there somewhere. Hiding in the Tartarus Zone. The way it spreads, and moves, it almost seems alive." Annie stared off into the darkness. It was actually so dark she couldn't be sure if it was the right direction, but it had to be one of them. "We were stuck in Parole this whole time and we didn't know."

"And you're starting to think it was better that way, huh?"

"I don't know." She shook herself away from the horrors in her imagination, and made herself focus on his face, lit up in the stark glow of the proximity ward circle. "I'm still glad we got out. I just didn't expect..."

"You thought the world outside would be safe." Ash's eyes dropped for a moment. "You deserved better. Well, we're working on it."

"Not your fault," she said with a mirthless little laugh. The whole situation was almost absurd. Either laugh or cry, and she was all out of tears. "Who knew it was like this? A poison wasteland—and Eye in the Sky is out here too? Run by a guy even worse than Turret?"

He didn't reply.

"Did you know?" she asked again after a few seconds, almost afraid of the answer.

"We had suspicions," Ash answered slowly, as if measuring his words. "Major Turret's focus was always on Parole, yeah. But we could tell we weren't his only target. Our agents in SkEye, like your mom and dad? And the FireRunner crew... we saw enough to know something was wrong."

"And you didn't tell me."

"Why would we rip that hope away from you?" He frowned,

shoulders bunching up with sudden tension. "Sometimes, hanging onto blue sky and sunshine is all that keeps people alive."

"I would've liked to know." She folded her arms. "I always want to know the truth."

"Yeah, I know." Ash sighed, slumping forward a little. "I'm sorry. I was hoping... I don't know, somehow things would be better when we finally got everybody out. We'd have it more under control. Look how well that turned out."

"It's worse than you expected?"

"We knew *something* happened ten years ago, around the time Parole got cut off from the rest of the world. A huge explosion, a blast like... not a nuclear detonation, but similar. It poisoned basically the entire midwest. We didn't know how bad it was." He folded his hands and stared at them for a few seconds. "Or what was inside."

"Ghosts aren't supposed to be real." Annie shivered.

"A lot of things aren't supposed to be real, but look where we come from. And the Tartarus... *things* aren't really ghosts," Ash said firmly. "People just call them that because they like being dramatic. They don't think, they're not even alive, and they probably never were. They're not animals even, they're just—try not to think about them."

"It's all I can think about, ever since Dr. Cole's last broadcast, about how she thinks they're communicating. With each other, and—"

"Okay, great." Ash's smile turned slightly more obviously nervous. "I'm telling you, the wasteland wildlife is not high on our list of concerns. Just try to forget 'em, okay?"

"I'm trying. I'm glad we have shields at least, but it'd be nice to have more ways to fight back. Or find our family and friends or do just about anything."

"Well, we got two flash-cans right in that bag, and once we get to Meridian, I bet Dr. Cole will have a ton more, since she pretty much invented them. Seriously, just focus on Meridian first. Then Parole. Get there, get home, rebuild, defend." A thoughtful look crossed his face. "Speaking of, when we get home, remind me to find Liam, wherever he got to. I mean, for once, the Turret House might be a good thing. Assuming it's still standing, that place has to have some serious defenses."

"Aw, Ash, I said our *friends*."

"Hey, he's not such a bad guy. He made some bad decisions and—"

Annie made an extended gagging noise that demonstrated quite eloquently what she thought of Liam Turret.

"Okay, fine." Ash laughed, shaking his head. "You've made your point."

"Ugh, have I, though? I don't get why you let him keep coming around."

Ash shrugged. "The library's there for everyone. The front part, anyway. What's left of it."

"Exactly. He's just trying to get in 'cause he thinks it's a secret rebel base or something, he actually said that."

"It *is* a secret rebel base. Was. Will be again."

"Oh my God." Annie rolled her eyes. "You think we can trust Liam

Turret for one second? Really? His last name is Turret."

"His mom was an old friend," Ash said simply. "We trusted her."

"Just cause his mom was a good person doesn't mean he is. Look at his dad. That guy's just gonna end up stabbing us in the back. He already thinks he's too good for us and looks down his nose at everyone."

"Mm." Ash nodded. "He could use an attitude adjustment. A big one. And I can't really think of much that'd help more than getting out of that big creepy house, away from the Major. Libraries are good for that. Anyway, people come from all over Parole for a safe place, why not from the most dangerous of all?"

"'Cause he's up to no good," Annie grumbled. "And he's a snob. And he looks at me like I'm gonna just automatically get into some kind of shenanigans, like everything's so freaking scary outside his little bubble—and he looks like somebody who'd use the word 'shenanigans.'"

"Oh, come on Annie. For real. Look in my eyes," Ash grinned, waving grandly toward his own face. "You really think I can't handle one cranky noodle? If he decides to do the dumbest thing in the world—stab us in the back, sneak anywhere he shouldn't be, mess with you—he's the one who'll regret it. But he won't."

"Because..."

"Because I've been taking in stray dogs all my life and they have two different looks. Alley hounds—survivors—and lap babies."

"Seriously?" Annie groaned. "Ash please. Don't say—"

"Now your alley hounds are gonna get mean and hard and do whatever they gotta do to stay alive, and they're the ones who are gonna make it in Parole, just like people. That's why I told you to leave any dog you see running around outside alone, just leave it to me, because—"

"It'll be used to the fire," Annie sighed. "It'll be scared to death of humans, it might be sick or wild and ready to bite anything that comes close."

"Right, good!" He gave a satisfied nod, clearly on one of his favorite subjects. "Those are the only ones left. But the ones at the library, any actual pets left here... lap babies. Cuddlers. They need human love and affection and wouldn't survive five seconds out there."

"So you're saying Liam... isn't an alley hound." Annie refused to voice the alternative.

"Hey, I actually saw him smile the other day. Did you know he can?"

"Bullshit."

"It's true. And watch your language."

She muttered something.

"What was that?"

"I said I'd rather watch my language than any more weird, awkward flirting."

Ash opened his mouth but no words came out at first. When they did, he stayed facing away, expression kept carefully serious. "I don't know what you're talking about, but even if I did, I'd be—*yes?*" Now he looked, in time to catch her laughing.

"I said I changed my mind, I *do* know why you let him keep coming around."

"No—I do not—that's completely—I am *done*," he made a decisive swooping motion with both hands and turned around again. "When you're ready to have a mature conversation that isn't—*this*—I'll be right here."

Laughter subsiding, Annie relaxed into a quiet much more comfortable than she would have thought possible just a few minutes ago. All of the harrowing week's anxiety faded here in the circle's soft glow.

"Hey," he smiled again, and at least on the surface it didn't look like an effort. "Ever think you'd be two thousand miles away from Parole? I sure didn't."

"I always knew we'd get out, but actually being out... it just feels different." Maybe she should have been proud. But somehow that knowledge didn't make her feel brave or triumphant. It made her feel exposed, vulnerable, very small. "Mom's always saying getting out's the goal, it's where we'll be safe, we just have to get out. And Dad's like, OK great, that's the first step, but what's the next one, what comes after that?"

"And they're both right. Tam's got the immediate small picture, Duy's got the big picture, extended plan. Now we're out, so the first step's done. And the big picture is just... same as before. Stay alive, stay one step ahead of SkEye. Do what we can for Parole from the outside. Get everybody back together, so we can all go home again and get on with our lives."

"Yeah."

"Yeah?" He raised his eyebrows in concern at the tired flatness in her voice.

"Okay." She wasn't panicked, didn't have the desire to pick at her hair. She just felt hollow. "Just can't stop thinking about them."

"They're fine. Listen," he said in a softer voice than before. "Your parents are both fine. I know it sounds totally back-asswards to even think, but undercover in SkEye is literally the safest place for 'em right now. They've built a life there learning how to deal with that freaking place, how to move in SkEye's circles without getting caught, how to listen and watch and keep all of us alive. They're not just taking care of each other, they're the ones who are gonna be holding Parole together for—"

"I know!" It came out louder than she intended, more desperate. "Sorry, I'm just—I don't want to hear that it was smart, or the right thing, or that they love me and want what's best for me, or any of that! I just..." she trailed off, losing words faster than she could find them. The more important the words, the faster they disappeared like dry sand slipping through a tight fist.

"You just want your mom and dad."

"Mm-hmm." Her shoulders dropped along with her head. Suddenly she felt as if she'd run those two thousand miles. "I miss them so much. I worry about them all the time, like now that I'm not there, something bad will definitely happen."

"I hear you." He shook his head. "Them staying, you going with me—the plan wasn't always... unanimous. But I'm telling you, we did plan for exactly this. Doesn't make it better, I know. And it's fucked that they had to think about it at all. But the best way to make it up to them is to take care of yourself and stay safe, that's what they want." He cracked a smile at her. "That part was unanimous."

She was quiet for a long few seconds, staring into the jar of fluid. It was getting darker but she could still make out the outlines of the pancreas. Somehow the shape was comforting, but made her chest ache.

"I've never *missed* so many people before. I just wish..."

"Hey, we'll find that heart. We'll put 'em all back together again, good as new. Parts and people."

"I keep thinking about Rowan too." Again she felt the strange pang of mixed comfort and sadness. "It's weird to think about them being out here too, on a big ship instead of the library."

"Yeah, I know." From the way Ash's smile faded, she guessed he felt the same. "Or the library not being there when we get back. But it will be again. I don't know if I've always been the best brother, but I can do that. Rebuild the library, get our home standing again, and then get everybody back together in it. You and your parents, Rowan, Zilch..."

"Rowan is gonna be so happy when we get back with Zilch's pancreas—and heart," Annie said, chest filling with warmth for the first time in far too many cold, fearful nights. "Cause it's proof they're safe, you know? As long as these things are alive, Zilch is alive, right? Even if we can't find Zilch, we can do that."

"Yeah, we can." Ash's face softened into a smile. "You know, you're right. This has been hard on all of us, but God—the library, then Zilch, then... just remind me to check on the goat-sib when we get home.

About time they caught a break."

"And once we find Regan, things will really get better. Like how they're supposed to be." She couldn't remember the last time she'd felt so energized and hopeful. It was amazing what just the smallest win could do. "He's out here somewhere, we know that much."

Ash nodded, and if he hesitated or didn't make eye contact, Annie didn't pursue it. "Sure looked that way from the footage I saw."

"If anyone escaped from Parole, it's him," she insisted. "He'd never get stuck back there, not if there was a single way to get out."

"Well, he always was good at disappearing." Annie looked up in time to see Ash's eyes slide away and slightly out of focus. "Listen, I know you've got questions, about why Regan disappeared... and then left. I've got them too, Garrett wouldn't j—" He stopped mid-word and looked away.

"Ash?" She pressed, puzzled. "Wouldn't just what?"

He turned back to her slowly, and seemed to very carefully measure what came next. "Losing Garrett Cole was... a blow. But not everything adds up. I don't know what happened, but finding Regan would be a good start."

"Yeah," she tried to sound happier than she was, still feeling oddly shaken at the way Ash's eyes had so suddenly hardened. What could have upset him so much, mentioning Regan and Garrett in the same sentence? "Like... maybe that recording wasn't what it looked like. Maybe Regan didn't really just leave without saying goodbye."

"At the very least, we can ask him when we find him." Ash shook off his increasingly grim glower and gave her a more level look. "My theory? He's after the same thing we are. Zilch's heart, just didn't slow down to explain. Can't blame him."

Annie only realized she was smiling when she felt it creeping across her face. They didn't come close to the most unconventional family in Parole, even including everyone in the library, scales, horns and all. People connected wherever they could, and in each other found community, hope and life better than mere survival. And small moments like these reminded her of how deep connections and understanding ran, and how glad she was that her definition of 'family' included him.

"Thanks. I hope that's it. I just want us all to be back together again, that's all."

"Me too."

When she thought about Parole, she was torn in two directions. Home, and nightmares. Comfort, relief, love—and falling, fire, horrors, loss. But when she thought about the people who lived there, she felt only warmth, and never a burn.

"Listen, Ash, I know you didn't want me out here. And I didn't want to leave. But once I was out? Nobody ordered me to go on this mission, I volunteered." Annie's hands balled into fists and new determination entered her voice. "I'm the fastest driver in Parole or out, and everybody knows it. Even Finn finally admitted it," she grinned. When he didn't return her smile, her eyes went hard again. "If we want to get all the way to Meridian and back—alive—I'm the best chance we got and you know it."

Before either could continue, an eerie sound rose up around them, a wailing somewhere between a wounded cat and a despairing human. Many voices out in the darkness beyond the alarm circle's light. "Ghosts."

"Oh, yeah, they're out there tonight," Ash said, nodding and sounding entirely unconcerned. "They sure are out there."

"Flash-cans are in the bag, right?" Annie shot a glance toward the packs sitting at the edge of the light cast by the glowing proximity ward ring.

"Yeah, got 'em right... hey." Ash's voice softened. "If the ghosts are yelling their heads off somewhere out there, it means they're not sneaking up on us here. Let 'em have a party out there, we're fine."

"Sounds like there are a million of them." She shivered, listening to the far-off wailing.

"Don't worry. If a ghost does give us a hard time, all we gotta do is lay the smackdown once, then that's it. Convenient."

"Cause it'll run and tell its friends?"

"Not to mess with us, yeah." He nodded easily. "But they won't. They're just gonna hang out way out there and yell for a while. It's what they do."

Parole had never been quiet. The roar of the fire was constant, accompanied by thrumming helicopter blades and screaming sirens—and occasionally screaming people. Crashes, crumbling ground, explosions, destruction. But nothing like these unearthly shrieks, clicks, and almost metallic-sounding keening. Nothing about these cries carried on the wind sounded human. "Ash, do you ever regret leaving Parole?"

"Wow, what brought that on?"

Annie stared at him as the ghosts wailed. Coming from anyone else, the question would have been sarcastic. From him, especially when he spoke to her, it wasn't. Like her, Ash had never developed a Chrysedrine ability, but readily accepted and fiercely protected Parole and all its fantastic elements as his home and family. Still, sometimes his level of acceptance of things that would and probably should bother anyone else could border on the fantastic alone.

"We finally escape, and it's a poison wasteland outside. And it's full of ghosts that change shape and whisper to you, and everything's trying to kill us, including other humans. And that wasn't an answer."

"No, I don't regret it," he said, and like always, she believed him. "Godfather job description includes protecting you during apocalyptic disasters. If I regretted that, I'd fire myself. Besides, we gotta get to Meridian and whatever genius stuff Dr. Cole dreamed up to save the world. And Zilch's heart is out here somewhere. Regan too. We find them, we bring 'em home."

She listened to his words and tried to hear. But above them the far-off cries echoed until they sounded like they came from right outside the circle of light. It was never fully dark in Parole. The fire's glow was omnipresent. Once the sun went down, the darkness almost became a tangible thing she could reach out and touch. Something that might suffocate them along with every single little light in the defensive ring, the only thing keeping them safe. Annie didn't even realize she was shaking until her teeth started to chatter.

"Hey. It's okay." Ash opened his arms and she immediately pressed in close, tucking her head beneath his chin. "We've gotten through way worse binds than this."

"I know. It's just... ghosts. What are we supposed to think when they scream like that?" She clenched her teeth together, tried to stop shaking.

"It's just Tartarus trying to scare you." Ash's voice drowned out the otherworldly shrieks from somewhere in the inky darkness so thick it almost seemed tangible itself. "Tartarus lies. It gets in your head, digs out what it thinks will make you stop running. Then it takes what's inside, and puts it outside. That's all ghosts are. Things that make you stop running, and look back. So don't listen to them. You're not going that way."

"I know," she said again, eyes tightly shut, trying to block out everything except his words and the vibrations of his voice in his chest. "They're not real. They're just like Sharpe, they're trying to make me stop. I won't stop. I won't ever stop."

Ash never seemed to have trouble sleeping. It was a gift. Not a Chrysedrine-granted ability, but one of the sweetest mercies somebody could possess in Parole. The ability to simply shut your mind off, detach from the horrors around you, and go somewhere else for a few hours. Not many people could in that city. Parole was full of insomniacs, and even more nightmares. A lot of them didn't go away when you woke up.

Annie didn't have that gift. She spent most of the night staring at the sky, caught halfway between marveling at the blanket of stars, so bright and brilliant she could hardly believe they were real—and trying not to think about *why* she could see them.

They were so alone. So small. Tiny little bugs on the edge of the Tartarus Zone, a terrifying wasteland that moved and changed. She never thought she'd find a place more full of ghosts than Parole, but here it was. She never thought she'd want to go home so badly. Never thought she'd want to get back in once she got out.

No ghosts actually appeared that night, except the ones in her head and heart. Annie barely slept, but when she did, she found herself in a familiar and comforting place. She'd seen it many times before in her dreams, and like every time before, she wasn't alone.

They'd made tire-tracks across another couple hundred miles of poison-wracked wasteland by noon, while the sun beat down mercilessly overhead. No shade except helmet visors cut the harsh glare of the road. The brightness was a reminder of the blast ten years ago that had destroyed the ozone layer, and there wasn't so much as a cloud overhead to filter out the harsh UV rays. Even the outskirts of the Tartarus Zone were an endless sea of darkness at night, and an unforgiving desert during the day.

Then, something broke the empty line of the horizon. A full mile behind the speeding motorcycle, but in a clear and unbroken line of sight, a long, thin shape like a telephone pole rose over a rolling hill and kept rising.

"You're seeing that, right?" Annie asked without turning around or breaking her speed or rhythm for a moment. Her in-helmet display locked on and projected more metal shapes as they came into view over the top of the hill. From this distance it looked like a crow's nest and ship's rigging cresting a steep wave in a building storm. Panic surged through her like an electric current and she opened up the throttle, picking up speed and leaning forward.

"Just fly steady." Ash's hands were on her shoulders, gave them a squeeze. She focused on the familiar nine-fingered pressure, used the feeling to ground herself. Breathe against it. Keep breathing. "Sharpe wants us to see him because he thinks we'll quit thinking and start panicking. He's just trying to scare us—"

"It's working!"

"You got this. Shields?"

"They're up, full strength," she confirmed with a glance at the faint shimmer like a soap bubble that surrounded them, easy to miss unless you were actively looking for it.

"Good. Now don't look back."

If she didn't before, she had to now. She'd been right to compare the rising shape to a crow's nest, because now, she could see their pursuer clearly: a huge metal craft, a military-looking vessel that should have been cutting a wake through ocean waves, or firing off rows of artillery. Instead, it floated around twenty feet above Tartarus' scorched earth, rising over the crest of the hill as easily as if it were still out at sea—coming after them with surprising speed.

"He's locked weapons on us," she said, voice tight, as her display surrounded the ship in warning lights. A line of red text began to flash: *CONFIRMED THREAT DETECTED.*

"It's okay, we've still got shields. Just look for a way to lose him."

Black sails rose, unfurled against the bright blue sky. The gravity-defying, speeding ship couldn't possibly need them to propel itself forward, and there was no wind even if it did, but they blotted out the sun—and a black flag rose high. Emblazoned on it was a white shape. Not a pirate's skull and crossbones, but inflicting the same immediate dread. She didn't need to magnify the view, but couldn't help it. An awful, morbid need for confirmation made her focus and zoom on the flag anyway, and shudder at its symbol. A white shark's fin.

"Annie, hey, listen to my voice," Ash said almost conversationally. "There's nothing behind you. You pass it, it's gone. Nothing exists except the road ahead."

"He's gotta still have Zilch's heart," Annie whispered, eyes flicking up to the 'rearview-mirror' display of the ship in her helmet. "We have to turn around. Face him—"

Bang.

The gunshot sounded like a far-off thunderclap, and there was a delay of almost a half-second before impact. It slammed against them broadside like a cannonball, the energetic shielding absorbing and distributing the force. They both clung to the bike as it pitched sideways, nearly tipping over. Ash yelled something in her ear but she couldn't understand, all that existed in Annie's world now was getting them right-side up again and keeping moving, a moving target was harder to hit, and they were a target now—

Then the shields flickered and crackled in a wave of static electricity that sent shivers down both their spines. Annie felt like her hair was standing on end even inside her helmet. Then it disappeared. The static, the shield, and every thought in her head.

No words. White noise. Shields gone. Exposed. Pirate-ship with shark flag behind them. Gunshots. Wind. Road still whipping by below them but she wasn't there.

"No blood in the water today." Ash's voice brought her back to the present and she remembered words existed.

His arms wrapped around her completely and she felt a soft tap as his helmet rested against the back of hers, a reminder he was real, he was here. She was driving, both their lives in her hands—Zilch's life, everyone's in Parole if they never came home—but she wasn't alone. She held onto his voice the way he held onto her, even as the terror of the shark-fin symbol burned into her brain like a red-hot iron.

"Come on, stay with me! He doesn't have us yet!"

"Okay." Annie's dry throat hurt when she swallowed; she used that to stay grounded too. She blinked hard, but it wasn't to fight back tears. The motion shut off her in-helmet displays, and the huge enemy ship disappeared from view. "Nothing behind us."

"Attagirl. Now we got a good lead. We're out in the open here, but see those trees? They're gonna get thicker. Past that, hills. Past that, I don't know, a riverbed, a ridge, a town, something."

"There's always something." She forced the words out. She forced them to exist.

"That's right. You can lose him. You can do this, Annie."

"Especially if we go off-roads." She clenched her teeth so tightly her jaw began to ache. She thought about the chain around Ash's neck, the tooth on the end of it. She couldn't feel it, but knew it was pressed between them, somewhere against her back. What would an entire mouth full of those feel like, clenched? Open? Razor-edged and smiling? "Lifting off."

"Hanging on."

She flipped a small dashboard lever. The motorcycle's engine didn't rev or sputter—instead the roar fell to a soft hum, nearly inaudible over the sudden gust of wind. The biggest change was that their motion was now much smoother. Tartarus' poison spread tended to eat up the asphalt, so the roads cutting through its expanse were rough. But even here, air was a gentler ride than pavement.

"Okay," Annie said resolutely. She didn't look back, but she glanced down with a satisfied nod as they rose into the air. The huge wheels had rotated and pulled up into the motorcycle's chassis; all systems go. They flew around ten feet above the road, speeding along much faster than two or three wheels ever would have been able to carry them. Now they had a chance. "If he's gonna catch us, he'll have to work for it."

"He won't catch us." Ash's voice was grim, and she couldn't help but shiver. No, the man in the ship behind them had no intention of catching them, or taking them alive. "He'll never get close enough. Up there. "

Annie followed the squeeze of his hand on her right shoulder to see what appeared to be towering, dark cumulonimbus storm clouds on the horizon—and rapidly getting closer. These clouds stretched all the way to the ground in a solid wall, obscuring everything behind a curtain of ominous vapor thick as the smoke they'd left behind in Parole. Flashes of lightening came from far away behind them, but getting nearer all the time. As fast as the bike was moving, the storm was rushing to meet them.

"Tartarus," she whispered. "I thought we weren't going near the actual edge."

"So did I," Ash answered grimly. "Remember when I said the borders move around?"

"Yeah. Helmet filters on?"

"That'd be good. Don't worry, even without a shield, they'll hold up for a full day."

"How about the engine, you tested it for this?" She focused on the words, procedure, not the reality of what they were about to do. If she thought twice, she might not be able to do it.

"Should be fine. But we won't be in this stuff that long, just enough to lose this shark."

Annie nodded, took a breath, and opened the throttle all the way. "Going in."

They cut away from the highway and lost the shark. Visibility was next to zero in the storm bank, but there was nothing to run into in the open wasteland. Still, it felt like driving blindfolded, and Annie couldn't tell if they were still being chased. Not until they emerged from the thick mists to find Sharpe's ship gone, the area around them empty once more. She'd never been so glad to leave anything behind. Not since the fires of Parole. But unlike Parole, she knew she wouldn't have a strange, conflicted desire to return.

It had only been around ten minutes according to the in-helmet and dashboard clocks, but it still felt as if they'd spent the entire day in the disorienting fog. Just like how Annie knew intellectually that her helmet filters would keep her from breathing in any poison, but when she saw the Tartarus clouds, she had to concentrate to keep from instinctively choking anyway.

Night fell, cold and surprisingly fast as always out here, and they were both relieved to find a small town interrupting the arid expanse. Somehow the small collection of buildings seemed even more 'in the middle of nowhere' than unbroken wilderness. It was deserted, as small towns that fell in the Tartarus Zone's outer reaches often were. Nothing lasted long out here.

Each vacant building looked equally dark and silent, but Ash advised her that an empty garage and auto center seemed the most sensible—and not because their ride needed a refill or repair. The large motorcycle wasn't just fast, or advanced, but incredibly durable. Annie imagined she could drive it directly into a wall, and drive it away again with only a couple scratches. And although Danae's expertly-crafted creations generally ran on Parole's toxic fumes instead of gasoline, apparently Tartarus vapors also made for good fuel. This location was strategic. It was on the edge of town for an easy exit, and the windows in the interior hallway gave a good vantage point down the main street. This town had been abandoned for a reason.

"How far to Meridian now?" Annie called, setting a proximity alarm sensor on the floor in the center of the doorway in which she crouched. The hall beyond was dark and still as the rest of the town. She didn't trust it for a second.

"'Bout a hundred miles, if I'm right about where we ended up," Ash said from across the small room where he was placing alarm sensors as well. Setting up the ward circle had become a nightly ritual that both of them almost enjoyed, something to make the night less threatening.

"That's nothing." She smiled for the first time since they'd lost their protective shielding. "We could've made it before dark."

"The way you drive? Yeah, probably. But better safe than sorry." He turned away from the single window, satisfied with the sensor placed in the center of the sill. "Night comes faster than you think out here. If we're still on the road when it's dark, especially without a working shield, we'll be sorry."

"Okay, so tomorrow morning for sure." But her confidence wavered, and concern crept back into her face and voice when she looked up again. "I thought that shield was supposed to handle just about anything. And it gets taken out by a bullet?"

"It's... just the effects of being out here this long," Ash said slowly, and she could tell he was figuring it out as he went, just like she was. "The Tartarus Zone atmosphere is corrosive, even this far away. It breaks down machinery, and shields, I guess, over time. It's been what, a week since we left the FireRunner? Long enough to weaken the shields for a bullet to punch through."

"Okay, great. And we're breathing this stuff that's so poisonous it breaks down advanced shielding tech. Wonder what it does to lungs."

"Never been a poisoning case that wasn't from direct storm exposure," Ash said with an easy shrug. "But yeah, we can turn on the filters from here on just in case, especially now that it's moving around on us. We'll still make Meridian by tomorrow, though. Even with today's... excitement, we're actually ahead of schedule—knock on wood," he said, tapping a quick shave-and-a-haircut on the windowsill.

Annie stamped twice on the hardwood floor too. "Not just a saying anymore, huh?"

"Nope. Been years since I've seen so many..." Ash put his hands on his hips and eyed the floor, the dusty blinds, the small bits of paper in the corners. "Fire hazards."

"Feels kinda good, though." Annie had to smile. "Light 'em up?"

With the glowing ring around them, as always, she breathed easier, felt safer.

"Good." Ash turned around slowly, giving the unbroken ring of light a satisfied nod. "Room's a little smaller than I usually set up in, but it'll do just fine. I can take on any solid nasty in a room this or any other size. If it's got a pulse, I can take it down."

"I don't want it to come to that." Annie's eyes flicked down to Ash's left hand, lingered on the third finger with its missing second and third joint. "Ghosts suck, but..."

"But Sharpe has a pulse and he can do serious damage." Ash just said it without hesitation, and held up his hand. Used it to wave at her. If it was anybody else but him, Annie would have been embarrassed she'd been so un-subtle. Instead, she just shrugged and nodded. "Well, I can do serious damage right back to him. And he knows that."

Ash picked up the chain he wore around his neck and swung the shark's tooth on the end back and forth, dangling it at her and grinning behind it.

"I know it too." She jammed her hands in her pockets so he wouldn't see them shaking, and she wouldn't feel it as much. "Still, I... we already have too many missing pieces."

Ash's smile faded. He let the chain, the tooth, and his hand slowly drop. "Listen, Spark Pl... Annie. Yeah, you might lose some things out here. Sometimes the only thing you can do is take a piece right back from the guy who stole from you. Even if it's not the most even trade in the world. But I promise, I'm right here, and he is not getting his hands on you, or any part of Zilch, or anybody else we—"

"That's not what I mean." Her flat, quick interruption almost surprised herself. So did the words themselves. "I've been thinking. Sharpe does have a piece of Zilch. What if he has... other missing pieces?

Our pieces."

Ash glanced at his hand, then back at her. "You lost me there."

"He might have Regan too."

"No," Ash said without hesitation, shaking his head. "No, that's impossible. He doesn't."

"We know Regan's out here somewhere. So is Sharpe. And you said Turret's the one who wanted Zilch's organs, Sharpe's just delivering them—*and* we know Turret wants Regan more than anyone. So who's to say he didn't get to Regan before we could—"

"No," Ash said again, more firmly this time. "Listen, Annie, there are some things in this world I'm not even gonna think about. We lived in Parole for ten years, that should tell you something about what I'm *not* willing to imagine."

"I was just—"

"Sharpe getting his hands on my family is one of them, and Regan's family as much as you are. That—*man*, having a *piece* of Zilch was bad enough. He *does not* have Regan ag—" Ash cut himself off. His voice was often warm, often laughing, and more frequently, now, warning. It wasn't often cold, or hard. Now it was. Even though it wasn't aimed at her, Annie almost shivered again. Then realized something that made her blood run even more cold.

"Again?" she asked slowly. "Were you about to say he doesn't have Regan... *again?*"

Ash didn't answer at first, and he didn't look at her. He'd never lied to her, she was sure of it, and she trusted him not to start now. But she'd also asked exactly the wrong question—or maybe exactly the right one. She never found out.

A cold wind rushed through the room, and the circle of lights flickered as if they were candles caught in a storm.

Ash held up one hand and silently shook his head as she moved to get up. He slowly rose to his own feet, turning toward the open doorway and the sputtering light on its threshold. He answered her silent question with a slow nod toward the pack he'd brought in and placed against one wall, the one that until now had been an afterthought.

Annie reached for it—but froze before she made it all the way. A dark figure stood at the end of the long hallway. One she knew well. She stared at the wiry limbs, the subtle gleam of scales under the dim light of a streetlight from outside a window. Slowly, a smile spread across her face.

"Regan!" She cried, scrambling to her feet and rushing forward—until Ash flung an arm into her path, catching her across the chest.

"Easy, Spark Plug," he murmured, voice level as always, but now with a tight undertone of adrenaline. "That ain't our boy."

,Annie's mouth went dry. Immediately every bit of common sense and warning caught up to her and she sank back down to the floor. "Yeah..." The stranger was only halfway down the hall now. Much closer than a moment before. She didn't remember seeing them move. "They, uh... they can never get the eyes right."

It looked like Regan. It had the same long, pointed ears with their metal piercings, the same thin crest running down the center of its head, the same delicate frill of skin hanging from its neck. The same eyebrow ridges that came together in a quizzical expression he got when he was studying something that puzzled him, the same slight tilt of its head. Everything was familiar. Except for the eyes below the scaled ridges. Where they should have been yellow-gold with a thin vertical pupil, like a snake or cat's eye, they were entirely black. They did not shine like his, or anyone else's Annie had ever seen. Even when peoples' eyes—like Rowan's—were turned black by Tartarus exposure, they kept their shine; with these strange eyes, their matte surface seemed to absorb the light instead of reflect it.

"It's a ghost." Annie didn't have to say the words. She and Ash both knew. She said them anyway. It almost felt like self-punishment, for being foolish enough to almost run right into its arms.

"It sure is." Ash wasn't looking down at her with blame, or at all. Instead, he actually grinned at the thing that looked like Regan, but would never be. "And I gotta say, love what it's wearing!"

"What?" Now she turned to stare up at him, bewildered, sick. "It's wearing *his face.*"

"I know!" He said brightly, snapping his fingers. The ghost's scaly head followed the movement, attention rapt. The black eyes did not blink as Ash smoothly moved to stand between Annie and the hallway entrance, keeping up his unnaturally perky tone all the way. "Isn't that just terribly interesting? Get a flash-can ready, I don't know how long I can keep this thing busy."

Ash turned back to the ghost, snapping his fingers again, up and down, left and right, and 'Regan's' head followed every snap. Hyper-aware of her own movements, the chill in the air, the cold sweat running down her back, Annie slowly opened the pack and reached inside. She pushed past Ash's stash of close-range weapons: small guns, knives, metal knuckles. These would only help against an enemy with flesh and bone. Finally, she found what she was looking for, two baseball-like objects at the very bottom—

"Stop!" Ash barked and she looked up to see him holding very still across the room, hands up and knees bent as if attempting to calm a cornered lion before it sprang. "Don't. Move."

"Wasn't gonna." Her voice didn't shake, but it was close.

Between them, somehow, stood the Regan-ghost. It shouldn't have been possible, but like so much in their lives, it was. How had it moved past Ash's impenetrable defensive wall? It was like it had simply disappeared and reappeared in the center of the room. *It sure is a ghost, that's definitely the right name,* she thought, painfully aware of how easily visceral terror could become hysteria. *Stay calm. Just stay calm.*

"Good. No need to panic." Ash didn't move either, still half-crouched and at the ready, face set in a grim stare directly at the ghost—the only one who looked remotely calm. 'Regan' appeared expressionless and perfectly still. Unnaturally still. Staring directly at Annie.

"I'm not panicking." Annie never liked eye contact even with other people, but she wouldn't be able to look into these eyes if her life depended on it. More like holes than anything solid. More like empty space than anything alive. One look into those eyes in the face of someone she loved, and she'd freeze again. Anyone would. "But if you have a plan, I'd really... really like to hear it."

"Working on it," he said with only a slight raise in pitch and tension. "When I know, you'll know."

"Ghosts aren't supposed to come inside." She almost shook her head, then stopped the movement. "They never haunt towns. Even plague towns."

"Maybe this one likes the night life," Ash said, joke belied by his voice's sharp edge.

"Or maybe it followed us." She glared at one of the silent replica's hands. She knew those hands, the curl of the fingers and their small claws. It wasn't fair. Seeing Regan again after all this time, and it wasn't even him. Somehow it felt like a betrayal—not by him, by this place. Tartarus was showing her beyond all doubt exactly how brutal it really was. She wouldn't forget.

"That's a great thought, Annie," Ash said, still faux-cheerfully and painfully tense. "Let's think more about that awesome thought, after we figure out how to get this ghost to say boo."

Annie still didn't look in its face, but she could feel its eyes on her, its stare unbroken. This wasn't a perfect Regan copy after all. The outlines were familiar, but instead of green—vibrant and shining under Parole's layer of omnipresent grime—this specter was an ashen monochrome, made of starkly contrasting black and bloodless white. It did not seem to breathe, and cast no shadow. This could have been a projection, an image reflected in a greyscale mirror, with nothing to cast it. It didn't look *real*, more like a frozen image on a screen. Like encountering some kind of glitch in real life, something that should not exist, but did.

Just a ghost, she thought. One of many. This one just happened to look like someone she knew. But for all Ash had said they didn't think, they weren't alive, this one seemed fixated on her like it knew her too. Maybe it did. It must know appearing like this, like Regan, would get their attention.

"Ash?" Annie pressed after a few suffocating seconds.

"Window," he answered, pointing toward it not with his finger but clearly enough with his eyes and eyebrows.

"You want to climb out the window?" She almost forgot to whisper. Fortunately the ghost didn't respond. "That's your plan?"

"I want you out of this room with a ghost in it, yes," he said a little more exasperatedly.

"And then what? You're coming with me, right?"

"I'm fine with *me* in the room with a ghost." Ash's voice went softer, deadlier. "Not fine with you in it. Because when I'm done, I'm not sure there'll be a room left. But if you've got a better plan, I'm open to suggestions."

"Well, I've still got these." She glanced down at the small objects she held, but knew as soon as she spoke, that chance was long gone. They'd had a shot when the ghost was still at range down the long hallway, but flash-cans weren't meant to be used in a small room like this. Especially not with the target standing between them, very close.

"Good. Use 'em outside, where they belong."

"I'm not climbing out the window, Ash!"

"We're not arguing about this in front of the ghost!"

"I'm serious, I'm not leaving you—"

"*I'm* serious!" He glared at her, and she almost took a step back under the combined two stares. But she didn't. "I want you out of here now—"

"And I'm not leaving!" Annie shot back, not caring if her voice went above a whisper now. The Regan-ghost was already staring at her. "Unless you follow me out the window a second later! And you won't, will you? You gonna stay here and try to fight this thing?"

Ash didn't answer. Neither did the ghost, but she didn't expect that. Finally, she couldn't stand the nauseating stalemate a moment longer. Annie cleared her throat, and raised her voice.

"Hi," she said, looking directly into the ghost's empty eyes. She didn't blink.

"Anh Minh!" Ash's harsh whisper made her look, but only for a moment. He vehemently shook his head, long hair and shark-tooth necklace flying. The ghost with Regan's scales never took its hollow eyes off her, as if unaware Ash was there at all. "If this is your plan, find a new plan!"

"You were talking to it a second ago, why was that okay?"

"I was trying to *distract it*, not make friends—"

"I think it's trying to make friends with *us*! Why else would it turn into Regan?" She whispered back, then turned toward the familiar face with the alien eyes. "Do you want to talk to us?"

"*It's not him,* Anh Minh!" Ash insisted, voice rough, almost a growl even as he kept it low; it sounded like it hurt his throat. "It looks like Regan but it's not! You can't treat it like—"

She shot him a glare, and he closed his mouth, eyes widening in surprise. Maybe at her sudden intensity, maybe at himself and how quickly he shut up in response.

(*Every missing piece.*)

The words didn't come from either of them. And the ghost's mouth didn't move. Its voice sounded like a thousand whispers at once and sent more shivers down her spine than any ship in her rearview ever could.

"What?" Annie barely recognized her own voice. Or the laugh she realized came from Ash a moment later. It was so joyless, so full of loathing, that it didn't sound like something that should come from him at all. Nor did the bare-tooth grimace belong on his face. But she did recognize the words. "What did you just..."

"Told you," Ash snarled, mirthless laughter dying. "These things don't *talk*. All they do is mimic. It heard me say that earlier, just like it dug Regan out of our brains. That's not him—that's a giant parrot."

Annie ignored him, focused on the curious expression the ghost still leveled at her and tried not to think of it as a loaded gun. "Yeah, we've got a lot of missing pieces. Regan's one of them. Do you know who he is?" Nothing. Not a word, not a blink. She shot Ash another glare before he could interject. "Do you know whose face you're using right now?"

The ghost hesitated, seeming to struggle with the answer on the very tip of its long tongue. The way it swayed on the balls of its feet, fidgeted, fiddled with its pointed fingertips, the look of anxious, earnest, entirely Regan-like concentration, made her heart ache.

Finally, the ghost's mouth opened.

(*Good Night...*) the words were hushed, dry, distorted. They sounded nothing like Regan even under the garbled 'playback.' But she did know the voice. (*Dream Sweet...*)

"*Shut up!*" It wasn't a yell of fury. Ash's voice came out strangled, panicked, close to breaking. "That's not yours—you're not—"

Annie flung the flash-cans at the ground, directly at the ghost's feet, covering her eyes and facing the wall as they erupted into blinding white light. Wind rushed past her again, but hot this time, like the updraft from Parole's blaze, searing where it scraped her bare skin. Horrible shrieks filled the air, like a thousand tortured souls being exorcised from this small room. When they finally died away, so did the light. She opened her eyes to see Ash standing against the far wall shielding his head with his arms, before slowly lowering them as well.

"Sorry," she whispered. "I know these aren't for inside."

"It's fine," he whispered back, looking pale and clammy. "This is just... fine."

Shaking, Ash opened his arms and held them out. Annie staggered into them and they collapsed into an exhausted embrace, weak with both relief and post-adrenaline nausea.

"You were right." Ash's voice made her look up. For once it wasn't the steady reassurance she expected. It was tight, brittle, sounded every bit as unstable as when he'd heard familiar words—*Dream Sweet*—come out of the ghost's distorted mouth.

"What?" She couldn't remember what she'd been right about. Nothing felt right, now.

"They do communicate." He held her so tight it almost hurt, his hands shaking. Just when she was about to ask again, he opened his mouth, sucked in a breath he'd clearly forgotten he was holding. "But they're not trying to make friends. The song."

"I... oh. Oh, no." Cold dread started to build deep down. She knew what he was thinking, but didn't want to articulate it.

"Rowan's song." He spoke through clenched teeth, like every word was a labor to get out. "For Regan. From home. It was their voice. That thing knew..."

"It was in Parole," Annie whispered. Now she held him just as tightly.

"Yeah." There were many dangerous things out here. Ash's voice sounded like one of the deadliest she'd ever heard. "It wanted me to know. You were right, Dr. Cole was right, they're intelligent somehow, they're sending a message, and—"

"Wait. No. It doesn't mean a ghost was in the library," Annie recoiled from that terrifying thought. "We know they can read minds, sort of. It found Regan in my head. Maybe it found Rowan's song too."

"I don't know." Ash's arms tightened around her a little. "I haven't known shit since we left Parole. Nothing makes sense outside the bubble."

"Or..." She hesitated. Somehow even good thoughts seemed dangerous to venture. "Maybe Regan really is somewhere out here. Maybe it heard it from him."

"Maybe."

Annie didn't need to look up to feel Ash start to withdraw behind his high, thick walls, the kind you needed to survive in Parole. And outside it, it seemed. She buried her face against his chest, and the shark's tooth dug into her cheek. She didn't care, and pressed closer anyway. Annie held her breath, listening hard for the eerie keening that accompanied ghostly appearances. All she heard was the fast beating of Ash's heart, and her own. It filled her head, blocking out the sounds of her fast, shallow breathing, and the howling outside she told herself was just the wind nobody in Parole had heard in a decade. The perimeter circle lights had come back on, and remained steady and strong.

"Well, it's all clear now," Ash said after a few seconds. Simply, as if it wasn't the most terrifying and exhausting thing in the world to put one foot in front of the other. "Tomorrow, we'll get moving again. You said it before, these things are like Sharpe. Even if they're trying to communicate, they're lying, trying to get you to stop. And if you stop here..."

"We can't stop, ever. I know."

"So no matter what you see or hear, or who lies to you, or whatever ghost haunts you—or whatever face they wear when they do—you keep going. You run, you don't stop for anything."

"And you don't look back," she whispered.

"That's right. You're not going that way. Feeling better?"

"Yeah, we'll be fine." But she couldn't take solace in Ash's reassurance anymore—not when his heart pounded just as hard as hers. It hadn't slowed at all since the ghost had disappeared, didn't match his calm, steady words at all. For the first time, Annie began to doubt, and held on as tightly as she could. "Everything's going to be okay."

"That's the good word."

She'd always thought Ash wasn't afraid of anything. He'd always had the most easy, mellow-eyed smile even in the face of the most deadly danger. But how many years had his heart pounded like this, even as his powerful arms encircled her, shielded her and so many others from threats imagined and terribly real? Cold dread built in her stomach. It felt like looking into a ghost's eyes.

"Now, we might not have seen the last of Tartarus, but that's the last ghost we'll see tonight." He sounded so sure. She had never wanted so badly to believe him. It would have been so much easier to just accept his grown-up promise. Stay young, stay trusting. But she kept listening for that edge of anxiety, couldn't help wondering if she'd really heard it, or if it was just nerves. From now on, she'd always listen. "Next stop, Meridian. Then we'll really get some answers."

"Okay," she whispered, because she couldn't think what else to say.

She wanted to tell him that she knew how scared he was now, and that nobody should have to be brave all the time. It was too much to ask of one person. She wanted to tell him that she was scared too, and that whenever she needed to feel brave, there was a list of people she thought of, and his name was near the top. But the words wouldn't come. They were too important, she needed to say them too badly, so they got tangled in her head until they weren't words anymore, and she said nothing at all.

"Don't worry, I'm feeling lucky about tomorrow," he said, and she could hear the smile in his voice. "The way you drive, like a bat outta Parole? The miles will go by so fast, we won't even feel 'em. Just don't look back."

Annie's hands curled around the soft leather of his jacket like her fists around handlebars, and held on. "We're not going that way."

She dreamed again that night, but not of ghosts.

Nobody in Parole had seen a tree as big as this one in a long time, but she came here almost every night now. It grew on a ship that sailed over land, one that would never fly a black flag. These branches were filled with bright flowers that looked like stars so close she could reach out and catch one. Around and below, the darkness was soft instead of crushing, and she could hear the whisper of wind through the branches and the hum of a far-off engine. She smelled moist earth and metal instead of smoke, and when she saw three old friends sitting in the tree's spreading branches with her, she smiled.

"Welcome back," said Gabriel.

"There it is. Can you see it?"

"Meridian?" Annie focused on the faint glimmer of light on the horizon, flashing in the distance like a shiny quarter on a sidewalk. When she squinted, her helmet visor darkened in response, zooming in and enhancing the pixel-distorted resolution until she identified the far-off glitter, though they were still a few good miles away. It looked like a huge bubble, big enough to encompass a small town, but much smaller than Parole. "Got it."

"Told you I felt lucky about today." She heard the smile in Ash's voice again. "Just a couple more hours, then—"

He fell silent, and she knew. Just *knew* without looking, that the ship was there. The ship and its black shark-fin flag.

"It's him, isn't it?"

"Yeah."

"And we still don't have shields."

"No. Open her up."

She flipped the lever and the bike lifted off the ground. Annie leaned forward over the handlebars automatically, and felt Ash's hands tighten on her shoulders just like before. A moment later though, he wrapped both arms around her and his helmet hit hers harder than expected.

"Sorry, surprise hug," he said. "Just hold steady, okay? I'll try not to tip us over."

"He's gaining on us, isn't he?" Terror spread through her like a burning poison, her stomach lurched, and she almost gagged.

"Don't worry about Sharpe, just worry about the road," Ash said with a chuckle. It actually sounded real. Calm. "Keep an eye out for trees, ditches, anything. We're gonna make it, just breathe, okay?"

"Breathing, yeah, gotta breathe!"

"Good, so keep doing that. And keep running, no matter what." He paused, the space of a long, deep breath. Maybe he was following his own advice. His arms were tight around her and did not shake. "All right, Spark Plug, just listen to my voice, it's gonna be okay. Everything I said before, I meant. You're doing so good. I'm so proud of you, you hear me? I'm never *not* proud of you."

She could feel his heart pounding. *He's scared again,* she realized with a new flare of panic. *He's still trying to hide it but he's scared,* and so was she, so scared every beat of her heart and pulse of blood through her veins seemed to sting. The shark tooth dug sharp into her back.

"Just keep running, and no matter what, don't—"

Bang.

The crack of a sniper rifle rang through the air, so far-off it sounded like a distant firecracker. Not loud, not thunderous; it was almost anticlimactic. Annie kept her course steady, kept her eyes on Meridian.

Very slowly, Ash let her go.

His arms loosened their grip, fell on either side, and his body leaned away, shoulders dropping as if he were letting out a long, deep, exhausted sigh. She didn't need to see his face behind his helmet to know everything was wrong here, as wrong as the world outside Parole, and as broken as the shattered earth within it.

"*No!*" Annie's horrified cry ripped from her throat, loud in her own ears, ringing in her helmet. She twisted around to grab at him as he fell away—and seized the chain around his neck, hand closing around the shark tooth on the end. It stopped him from falling but he hung on the end of it like the tooth did, the thin chain all that was keeping him—

The chain snapped. She stared at the shark's tooth in her hand, its serrated edge digging into the flesh of her palm until it nearly drew blood. Before she could force herself to move, or even comprehend what was happening, Ash slipped from his seat and fell to the powdery earth.

Annie didn't know how she came to a halt or got off the motorcycle or if it was rolling or flying, or if it even stopped or kept speeding on without her. She didn't know if she was walking or running or sinking into the earth; all she heard was a rushing in her head and all she saw was Ash lying on the ground, very still, not right, not how people looked, not how humans were supposed to look, especially not him, wrong, wrong like the ghost, a glitch, a mistake in reality, she didn't have words for it, any of it. No words left in the world.

The sandy ground around him was beginning to turn red and wet. Like the outskirts of the Tartarus Zone, it was spreading, growing like a terrible stain. Something hurt her hand. She looked down. She still held the tooth, squeezed it too tight. Everything hurt. It was the only feeling.

Her knees started to shake as she leaned down. Saw herself reflected in his helmet as she reached toward it. Saw her own mouth open, saw herself try to form words, and fail.

Stopped.

(*You're not going that way.*)

Annie's head jerked up. She only realized hot tears were streaming down her face when she had to wipe them away to see the shadowy shape standing close beside her—very close. Nebulous at first, like a particularly fast-moving wisp of cloud, like an extension of Tartarus' storms itself. Then as she watched, it slowly resolved itself into a figure she knew, but not the one she'd seen last night. One with huge, spiraling horns.

"Rowan?" She whispered, numb, weightless, lost. Nothing made sense. The open sky stretched above and if she looked up she might fall.

The grey, ghostly figure with the all-black eyes stared at her steadily, like it was waiting for her to say what she wanted, or maybe for Ash to get up and speak. Somehow she'd expected another Regan, but now here was somebody else she loved. Someone she'd seen much more recently on the FireRunner. She couldn't take her eyes off the circular, ram-like horns, the goat-like hooves, the gently curious expression she'd seen a million times, like right now Rowan wanted her to explain a particularly odd teenage behavior or... Rowan's eyes had been black for years, but there was nothing real about these, nothing alive, or... she couldn't think.

Not with Ash on the ground. Who this monochrome figure with Rowan's face didn't so much as glance at. *Wrong.* This was wrong.

"You're not Rowan." Annie's voice shook now, her eyes burned, her throat wanted to close. She just wanted to get to Ash but she couldn't move a muscle. Not with those eyes that were *not* Rowan's on her. "You weren't Regan either. You're just a ghost."

Her eyes flicked down at Ash's still form, and the thirsty Tartarus earth around him. Cracks ran through his helmet. She fought to reach out, and to resist. The Rowan-ghost stared at her impassively, not once sparing a glance at the motionless body on the ground.

"Help us," Annie whispered, eyes staying on Ash once they were there. "You didn't hurt us when you were Regan. You were trying to talk to us. You're not evil, are you? Everyone thinks you are, but—"

(*Don't look back.*) The ghost spoke again. It sounded nothing like Rowan's gentle voice. Or Regan's. She knew it sounded very familiar but couldn't place the tone, not over the pounding of her own heart.

"I have to," Annie whispered. "I have to look back. I can't leave him here. Do you know who you are right now? Do you know the face you're wearing? This man is their brother. Do you know what that is, a brother? They're important!"

Slowly, the Rowan-ghost's head tilted in a quizzical gesture that was not at all their own. It was one of Regan's. Suddenly Annie wanted to scream. She was talking to a ghost—a pale mockery of reality, of the people she loved, something inhuman that would not understand. Maybe it couldn't.

"Do you know what family is? Do you know what love—or dying, losing, hurting... do you know what any of this is?" She was crying so hard now she could barely breathe. "Do you know why this—*hurts?*"

The ghost watched as Annie cried for a few long, terrible seconds. It watched as Ash lay still. Then it took one step. Not toward them, but to the side. Annie sucked in a terrified gasp, because the movement revealed a dark metal shape against the sky: Sharpe's towering ship, much closer than it had been before. She'd forgotten it existed.

A cold chill ran down Annie's spine, and the air rushed from her lungs. Somewhere, she knew Sharpe was lining up another shot. He never missed, even if he didn't hit what he was aiming for. Standing targets were easier to hit, and she stood very still, but every muscle felt locked in place. She couldn't move.

(*You're not going that way,*) the ghost whispered. Now she recognized its voice, where she'd heard it before, why it was familiar.

It was Rowan's shape, but Ash's voice. Annie shuddered, sobbing so hard she fell to her knees.

Then, the ghost turned away. It began walking toward the ship, silent hooves leaving no mark on the powdery earth. As it moved, it changed. With each step, the dark shape grew larger, shape elongating and twisting, until Rowan was gone, and something else entirely took their place. By the time its transformation was done, the ghost had become a dragon. An enormous, serpentine creature with a sinuous neck and tail ridged by spines that reminded her of Regan's neck frill and crest, and sweeping wings that blocked out the harsh Tartarus sun. The dragon leapt into the sky, hung for a moment hundreds of feet in the air, and dove directly toward the ship. The battleship almost jackknifed, rapidly changing course and firing off guns and heavy artillery. An intense and incredibly surreal aerial battle began... and none of it mattered.

Annie barely saw through her tears, and went numbly back to staring at Ash once she decided she wouldn't die in the next few seconds. Reached for him again. Stopped. Helmet. No. Needed to see him. But couldn't touch that helmet, couldn't take it off. Knew what she'd see if she did. Knew she'd never get it out of her head. Never be the same. Changed enough already.

No matter what you see, keep going. This place lies. It takes what's in your head and puts it outside. It tries to get you to stop, and if you stop...

She stood up but couldn't move. Couldn't stop staring at him.

Go. Go, dammit. Ghosts are helping. Won't keep Sharpe busy forever. Out here for a reason.

Annie forced herself to turn away.

Have one of Zilch's organ jars. Have to find the other one. Their heart. Save them.

She took a step.

Regan's out here. Find him. Save him.

Another step.

Get the data from Dr. Cole. Save Parole. Save everyone.

Step. Step. Run. Keep running.

Follow the dreams. Find Gabriel. Save...

Annie got back on her motorcycle and continued toward the shining spot on the horizon. Meridian.

She did not look back.

Acknowledgments

As always, thank you first to my parents for keeping me alive while I worked on this weird book, and thinking I'm putting good things in the world.

Thank you to Eri and Claudie, whose feedback is immeasurable and on whose feels I feed and grow strong.

Lyssa, as usual, made this book ridiculously pretty. Look at it. It's ludicrously pretty. What even.

And thank you to all of my incredible Patrons, especially Quinn and Dakota, for making more books like this possible!

About The Author

RoAnna Sylver writes unusually hopeful dystopian stories about marginalized heroes actually surviving, triumphing, and rocking really hard. RoAnna is also a singer, blogger, voice actor and artist who lives with family and a small snorking dog, and probably spends too much time playing videogames. The next amazing adventure RoAnna would like is a nap in a pile of bunnies. You can support more art and stories directly on Patreon.com/RoAnnaSylver!

Printed in Great Britain
by Amazon